AMISH LOVE SAVES ALL

AMISH PEACE VALLEY SERIES

BOOK 3

RACHEL STOLTZFUS

ISBN-13: 978-1545013984
ISBN-10: 1545013985

Download the Rachel Stoltzfus Starter Library for FREE.

Sign up to receive new release updates and discount books from Rachel Stoltzfus, and you'll get Rachel's 5-Book Starter library, including Book 1 of Amish Country Tours, and four more great Amish books.

Details can be found at the end of this book.

TABLE OF CONTENTS

ACKNOWLEDGMENTS

I have to thank God first and foremost for the gift of my life and the life of my family. I also have to thank my family for putting up with my crazy hours and how stressed out I can get as I approach a deadline. In addition, I must thank the ladies at Global Grafx Press for working with me to help make my books the best they can be. And last, I thank you, for taking the time to read this book. God Bless!

CHAPTER ONE

Naomi Miller leaned against the kitchen wall, shoving her hands into her neat, blonde bun, displacing the round ball of long hair. Tears streamed down her cheeks as she grieved for her best friend, Leora Lapp, who had been forced to watch her dat go into a mental hospital after trying to kill Leora and her mam, Lizzie. "Gott, why? They have done nothing to deserve this! Please, Lord, watch over all three of them and help Mister Lapp finally heal from all of his memories."

Finished with her quiet prayer, Naomi pulled her hair covering from her head and shuffled to the kitchen table, grabbing a napkin. She scrubbed her face clean of tears, and then blew her nose. *It wouldn't do for Dat or Mam to see me reacting so, or they won't let me continue working on the peer group.* Releasing a long, shaky sigh, Naomi exerted control over her emotions just as her mam came into the house.

"Naomi, what's wrong?" Annie's concern was evident on her round face.

"Nothing, Mam. I just came from seeing Leora."

"Ach, with her dat in the mental hospital, ja. How were she and her mam?"

"Upset." Naomi's voice quivered as she forced control over her vocalization. Exhaling slowly, she forced the sobs back again.

"Of course. Please let them know that I am so sorry for what happened." Annie glanced outside the large kitchen window, allowing the late-fall scenery to calm her spirit. "And you, my daughter. I know you're more upset than you are letting on. Go outside and take a walk. Your dat won't be home for a while— he'll be late for supper. I just got word from Deacon King."

"Oh? What is he doing?"

"He is working on presentation materials for our young teen couples. Go. Calm yourself down and come back in later. You do know that if he sees you so affected, he will take you off the peer committee."

"Ja, I know. We knew what was going to happen with the Lapps, but it was still a shock. Lizzie has to be so torn apart!"

"Ja, daughter, she is. But the English sheriff explained to her and Leora that a mental health placement is best for them *and*

Wayne. That, when he is discharged, he will be stabilized on medications and better able to control his moods and reactions to stresses."

Seeing it from that viewpoint, Naomi felt better. "And Lizzie was already working in the store, so it's not like she would have had to come back in, hoping there would be an opening waiting for her."

"Exactly. If you want to stay on the committee, child, you need to start looking for the silver linings. Go. Walk, then help me with supper."

Naomi's smile was much more heartfelt now. Grabbing her cape, she swung it over her shoulders and waved goodbye to Annie. "I'll be back soon."

Walking outside in the crisp fall air, Naomi thought about everything she and her mam had just discussed. *Ja, Lizzie and Leora were frightened and upset. They are going to miss Wayne. But it's better for them to miss him, knowing he's finally getting the help he's needed for so many years. And they are both working at the store, earning the money they need. I'll ask Mam to find out if they will need help with Wayne's carpentry orders. I am sure they hate having to ask once again.* Her thoughts veered back to the time, nearly a year ago, when Wayne had seriously injured his arm in a carpentry accident. The community's carpenters had lent their expertise and efforts in helping Wayne to keep up with his orders so he wouldn't lose customers and all of his tools. Shivering slightly in the chill breeze, she decided it was time to go back inside.

"Mam, what do you need me to do?"

"Hmmm, please make the dessert. Peach pie, I think. Then, take vegetables from the pantry so we can have them with the chicken."

"Should I make the potatoes?"

"Nee. I'm working on them now."

Looking down, Naomi saw that her mam had cut several potatoes into small chunks, along with most of an onion. "Mmm! Potatoes Anna!"

Annie smiled, her round face beaming. "Ja, I figured we could use some comfort-type foods. I know this whole thing has *ferhoodled* your dat because they have been friends for so long. What does Jethro say?"

Working on the piecrust, Naomi shook her head. "I don't know yet. All this happened after we went out last. I'm sure I'll hear from him and his parents about this. I do know they were really worried about Wayne. Then, when we learned he was planning to try and kill Lizzie and Leora, Mister and Missus Yoder felt so horrible, feeling like they had failed the whole Lapp family."

"But they didn't fail them." Annie worked on the chicken

and potatoes, deftly stirring the potatoes as she placed the chicken into the roaster. "If Wayne had been more direct about what was happening in his mind, we could have gotten to him and gotten help to him more quickly."

"I'm just grateful that we were able to do what we did." Naomi turned the peaches into the pie plate, on top of the piecrust. Sprinkling cinnamon on the peaches, she continued. "I was very surprised that the English sheriff and deputies were able to get to him as quickly as they did."

Naomi shivered before she could stifle the automatic reaction. Looking quickly at her mam, she smiled slightly when she realized Annie had caught her reaction. "Sorry."

"Why? We all saw something frightening. It's better to deal with it now than have it affect us for weeks down the road, ja?"

"Ja. I just don't want you and Dat to take me off the committee. That's all."

"So, you still want to work on it?" At Naomi's emphatic nod, Annie continued. "You can. As long as you are honest with your dat and me about how you feel about what we witness. This past Sunday was…horrible for all of us. We love the Lapps. Realizing that Wayne had fallen apart as much as he did frightened even the elders and the Yoders. I'm sure Jethro's parents will tell you that."

Now, it was Naomi's turn to gaze outside the large, bay

window. Seeing the leaves falling off the trees, she allowed the sight to help calm her spirit. "Ja, I'm sure. Mrs. Yoder looked…well, more than concerned." As the sky darkened, Naomi's mind went back to the lunch in their back yard. Seeing Wayne approaching Lizzie, a look of determination on his craggy face, had chilled Naomi. Shaking her head, she reminded herself of one thing: *We all knew what he had planned. And thank Gott that we had the assistance of the sheriff's department!* Remembering these two things, Naomi was able to calm herself down. "We had a lot of help. I'm keeping that in mind as I get over this. Mam, would you mind terribly if I went to visit Leora and Lizzie after supper?"

"Nee, as long as your dat has no objection. If you do go, don't be too long. And please, pass on our prayers and good wishes for them and Wayne."

"Ja, I will." Naomi worked in silence. Taking jars of vegetables out of the pantry, she brought them into the kitchen. "Beans and peas, I think. I know they're both green, but we have so much of them!"

"That's fine. They are your dat's favorite… Oh! There he is!"

Caleb walked into the kitchen, removing his black felt hat. Holding his cupped hands over his mouth, he blew into them, trying to warm them up. "It's getting cold out there!"

"Husband, I'm glad you're home! What did you and Deacon

King get done?"

"Some teaching materials that go along with our Ordnung. We've found that so many of our married couples and courting couples either believe the Ordnung doesn't allow our married women and teen women to work outside the home, or even that some of the men in the community are actually using the Ordnung to force their wives to stay at home, even as they know the Ordnung doesn't forbid wives working outside the home."

"I'm not surprised." Annie turned to check the chicken's progress, missing the way Caleb looked around the house.

"Ja, I truly thought our Ordnung would cause you to be brought before the community. Now that I know it doesn't, I am fine with your ownership of the Quilt Shop. And with Naomi managing it so you can work half-time."

Annie closed the oven door and wheeled around to face Caleb. Her eyes were wide. She had never heard that calm tone of voice coming from him in connection with her store. "Caleb! You're serious!"

"Of course! Seeing what happened with the Lapps opened my eyes to the dangers."

Annie quieted down quickly at that. "Are you saying…he may still be…?"

"Nee. But when he comes home, he will be watched closely.

Deacon King and the bishop are determined that this kind of thing won't happen again, ever."

***

As the Millers were recovering from the events of the weekend, John Andrews, whose family had moved to Peace Valley several years earlier, smiled, thinking of his girlfriend, Beth Zook. John had a hard time adjusting to his new community—as conservatively as the Peace Valley community thought, it was much more advanced than his Old Order Amish community.

John's smile slowly disappeared as he thought of Beth's consistent refusal to quit her job at the diner on the edge of Peace Valley. He rolled his eyes, thinking of her objections. *She says that she and her mam need the money they both earn. I am sure she could quit and, with a little budgeting, they would still be just fine. I am just going to have to continue working on her until she sees things my way.* John conveniently forgot that "working on her" included smacking Beth with a closed fist. As a farmer, he had become unusually strong, which he was willing to use against Beth's disobedience to his wishes. *I just have to strike her where marks won't show. Say, on her arms or her ribs. Soon, though, she will agree with me. I wonder what Mister Lapp did to convince his wife to quit her job…but why did she go back to that quilt shop? Does she care that she violates the Ordnung?* John was aware of the differences between the Ordnung from his old community—which was probably slightly more advanced than when he, his dat and mam had left—and that of Peace Valley. Still, he chose to discount the fact that he was thinking of the Ordnung that existed for his former community rather than that of his new home because it was something he was more comfortable with.

"John! Have you finished repairing the harvester?" John's dat, Big John, came into the barn on short legs.

"Ja, just a few minutes ago. I think it will be gut for next autumn."

"Gut. Come into the house for supper. I want to have devotions early so I can get to bed early."

"Ja. I will. I was thinking I could spend some time with a…friend."

"Hmm." Big John glared out at his son from under bushy, graying eyebrows. "Tomorrow's a working day. Ja, go on ahead, but be back here at a reasonable hour!"

John had grown up with those strict rules all his life, so he was quite comfortable with them. "Ja, Dat. I will." Hurrying inside, he barely greeted his mam, instead rushing upstairs to wash his hands and face. Coming back downstairs, he stood behind his chair, waiting until Big John was ready to give the silent prayer of thanks.

Mrs. Andrews silently and quickly served her husband and son their plates. Her husband had made it crystal clear at the beginning of their marriage that he expected this level of service at every meal. She was the last to sit and start eating. Out of long habit, she averted her eyes from both her son and husband, whose table manners were atrocious.

"Oh, wife, son is going out after devotions to spend a little time this evening with a friend. And he has promised he will be at home early, so we can start early tomorrow morning. As you know, John, though we may have harvested all our crops, the work still continues!"

"Ja, Dat. I will be home early and up at my usual time." John's voice, when he responded to his dat, was uncharacteristically modest.

"Gut, son." Big John continued to shovel large forkfuls of food into his mouth, barely giving himself time to chew and swallow.

"Hmmm. Apple pie. I was hoping for shoofly pie."

"I'm sorry, husband. I plan to serve that another night this week."

Big John sighed. "Okay, as long as you stick to that promise." He slowed down his chewing, fixing his gaze on his wife, Emma's, face.

Emma continued to get more and more nervous. Soon, she couldn't eat her pie because her stomach was twisted in knots.

She knew she would pay for this later in the week.

"Mam? Aren't you going to finish your pie?"

"Nee. I must have eaten so much I didn't leave room for dessert."

"Can I have it?"

"Ja, go ahead." Emma got up and began gathering her cooking dishes around the sink. She wanted to finish early so they would be on time for devotions.

John greedily grabbed the plate and finished his mom's pie in three quick bites.

"Wife, finish the dishes and clean the kitchen. We will have devotions in here and I want our setting to be appropriate for our discussion of Bible passages." Big John stood and, without thanking Emma for the meal, belched and went to relax in the living room.

As Emma worked to wash dishes and clean her kitchen, she stifled tears, wondering how her life had gone so wrong. Her dat had been strict with her and her sisters. But he had never been abusive toward them or their mam. Meeting Big John, she had been impressed with his ability to run a farm and coax the plants to grow. *Ja, we have had our rough years when, no matter his farming skills, weather conditions made it impossible for the crops to grow.*

After devotions, John left quickly to stop at Beth's parents' house. Standing at the door, waiting for someone to answer, he anticipated convincing her to quit her serving job. His smile creased his face as he anticipated her responses.

"Beth! I was hoping we could go for a buggy ride tonight."

Beth Zook gave a shy smile to John. Shaking her head, she said, "Nee. I am coming down sick and I'm responsible for taking care of mam. She's sick as well. And we both have to be well enough to go to work on Wednesday." She began to shut the door.

"I can take my chances," John spoke as he pressed his hand aggressively against the door.

Beth sneezed and coughed. "I'm sorry, John. I would love to go driving with you, but I'm running a fever. I can't leave mam."

John hated to be thwarted. Scowling, he allowed his hand to fall. Perceiving her refusal as deliberate disobedience, he allowed his hand to fist behind his back. Lashing it out fast, his fist connected hard with Beth's ribs.

CHAPTER TWO

Beth gasped and bit back her cry of pain. As she felt pain shooting from her ribs to her spine, she thought yet again about the peace she would have if she only had the courage to break up with him. "John! I'm sorry, but I can't go out. I have a fever and Mam does too. We need to recover. Please leave." Working up her courage, Beth stepped back and quickly shut the door. After making sure it was securely locked, Beth leaned weakly against the solid wood and allowed tears of pain and frustration to trickle down her pale cheeks.

"Beth? Daughter? Who was at the door?" Beth's mam was coming slowly downstairs.

Beth quickly wiped her tears away. Pulling a fresh tissue from the small package on the table, she blew her nose. "It was John, Mam. He wanted me to go riding with him, but I told him we are both ill. Do you need anything? Water?"

"I am getting some ibuprofen for my fever. You should take some as well. I do feel better, thankfully."

"Ja, I will take some, thank you." Beth's hand snuck under her crocheted shawl as she felt her painful ribs. She knew she would have a nasty bruise soon. Slowly, she moved with her mam to the kitchen, where she took their glasses out of the cabinet. "I'm just grateful tomorrow's our day off so we can continue   recovering."
"I know. We can't afford to take very many days off. But the owner won't allow us to work sick, either. I do wish…"

"What, Mam?"

"That we either got sick leave, or that I had confidence in my baking so I could work from home and earn the income we need. There's nothing I can say about Amos…Gott wanted him, so he's gone."

Four years earlier, Amos Zook had died after suffering from congestive heart failure for several years. "Mam, his heart just gave out. He was so tired at the end. I'm sure that, while he didn't want to leave us, he was also relieved. I would be, if I had been in his situation. And, about your baking…you bake beautifully. You could get the high prices some of our other bakers get for their products. I know it."

"Maybe. I just remember what Amos' mom said when she tasted my shoofly pie the first time. She said it didn't have very much flavor. When I tasted it, I wondered what she was talking about."

"What? She really must have loved a strong molasses taste or even the brown sugar taste. Any time I've tasted it, I loved the flavors."

"Ach. Well, she was the only fly in the ointment when it came to Amos and me. Well, other than his heart. But we knew as soon as we got his diagnosis that it would be just a matter of time."

This time, Beth couldn't hold her tears back. She missed her dat so much! Plus, her ribs were really sore and she felt horrible. "I'm sorry, Mam. I just miss Dat and I feel so sick."

"Let's go to bed, girl. That's the best thing for us right now—sleep."

The two women trudged slowly up the stairs so they wouldn't stimulate more coughing. In her bedroom, Beth removed her robe and lifted her gown. Looking at her ribs, she grimaced, seeing the bruise already beginning to bloom. She remembered how kind and gentle John had been at first—even if he seemed moody or angry at unpredictable times. His moods had served to keep her off balance. Of course, now she knew this. *If I could only predict when he's going to be in one of his moods!*

Sitting on her bed and sliding under the covers, Beth leaned against her pillow. She remembered the first time John struck her. They were coming home after the singing. It was supposed to be a celebration. They had been seeing each other—or "courting," as John still called it—for one year. Beth noticed he had been almost angry most of the evening. He wouldn't talk about it. But he said he wanted to spend more time with her after leaving the singing. She told him that she needed to be home right away because she was going…*wait!* Beth finally made the mental connection.

Every time she had work hours scheduled, he would get moody. It was her work the whole time! Her mind slowly took her back to that first time John had hit her. She had told him she had early working hours the next day, and he didn't like that. "I'm supposed to be your focus!" He practically screamed in her face. Then, his fist hit her arm, hard. She nearly fell out of his buggy. He grabbed her before she fell, and she was grateful…she thought. But he hit her again—this time in her stomach.

Beth came home and threw up almost in the hallway. She told her mam that she ate something that disagreed with her. *My Gott! He's serious! He doesn't want me to work.* She wasn't an able enough quilter, so she couldn't do that from home. She wished she had the courage to stop seeing him. Resting her hot forehead on her fisted palms, Beth began crying quietly.

The next day, her temperature was normal. Aside from some weakness, she felt normal again. "Mam, how do you feel?"

"Much better, denki! I just feel weak. Breakfast will help with that now that we can eat. Eggs and oatmeal, I think, with toast. Coffee?"

"Ja! I am so hungry!" But Beth was only able to eat a portion of what she normally ate. "I am so full. Are we ready to go now? We have to clock in soon."

"Ja. Let's just wash and dry the dishes. Why are you moving so carefully?"

Beth had been favoring her left side after being punched so hard the night before. "I don't know. Maybe I sneezed or coughed so hard that I pulled something." She now felt free to place her hand against her bruised ribs.

"Just be careful in the diner. You don't want to stress that any more."

"Nee!" Beth dried the dishes as her mam washed and rinsed them.

As they drove to the diner, Beth froze just slightly; she saw John in his dat's wagon. Turning away from the sight, she prayed he wouldn't see her. She knew she couldn't say anything to her mam. *I'll figure out a way of getting him out of my life. For gut.* Glancing in the direction John had been traveling, she let out a silent breath—he hadn't spotted them.

"Mam? When Dat got upset at you, how did he express it?" She held her breath, hoping her mam wouldn't figure out what had been happening.

"Did you and John have a disagreement? This is common with couples who are getting to know each other." Her mam seemed to be thinking back to her own courting days. "Well, our first disagreement was over whether I would work. He wanted me to stay at home and take care of the house and kinder. But he told me that, if we needed for me to work, he wouldn't stand in my way. In fact, after he took sick, he was the one who found out about the cook's position at the diner. He told me about it. 'You'd be perfect for it. Your roasts, chicken and vegetables top anyone else's in the community. And your desserts!' While I didn't feel very confident about my shoofly pie, he did. This was right before he had to stop working as a farrier. So the timing was just right. I applied and got the job." Her voice softened as she seemed to remember taking the job and, over the next year, seeing her husband's condition worsen. "He died a year later."

"I… I remember." Beth's voice was choked. "He loved you so much. And he supported my working as well. Do you think he did so because he could no longer work?"

"Partly, ja. But he was always somewhat forward thinking. While he would have preferred for me to stay at home, it didn't bother him that I liked working."

Beth remembered the scene at the Miller's several weeks earlier. "Ja. I thinking of the Lapps. Mister Lapp nearly killed Missus Lapp. Didn't he go into some kind of mental health place?"

Mrs. Zook thought for a few seconds. "Ja, something operated by both the Amish and Mennonites. At least he won't be made to give up his faith."

She shifted her position on the buggy seat, trying to ease the pain in her ribs. *I hope they aren't broken. He hit me hard enough.* As the morning wore on, it became harder and harder for Beth to hide her pain. Finally, just before she took her lunch, the diner's owner called her into her office. "Beth, you're obviously in pain. What's going on?"

Beth couldn't lie without being called out on it. Shifting on the kitchen chair in the small office, she opened and closed her mouth before speaking. "I…was hit in my ribs last night. My boyfriend." She flushed with shame. "Please don't tell my mam!"

The owner, an older, kindly Mennonite woman, opened her eyes in shock. "Beth! You need to be seen by the doctor! I'll send you—"

"I'll go, but please, Ann, don't tell Mam!"

"Beth, I'll keep your secret on one condition. *You* tell your mam." She waited until Beth nodded slowly. "Now, go. I'll call my doctor. He's the soul of discretion. Oh, and you need to make it clear to your boyfriend that physical violence against women is wrong, period. Promise?"

"Ja. Thank you. Can I come to work tomorrow? We need the money for bills."

"Only if you don't have broken ribs and can hold heavy trays of dishes." Ann stood. "Now, I have daughters of my own. Unpin your dress. I want to see the damage for myself."

Beth looked with longing at the door, just wanting to escape. With reluctance, she unpinned her dress and opened it, exposing the large, ugly bruise to Ann's view.

"Oh, my! You will be very fortunate if you don't have at least one broken rib."

Beth swallowed hard, trying not to cry. "What will you tell my mam? She'll see that I'm not here."

"That I sent you to run an errand for me. I'm not lying." Ann quickly phoned her doctor's office. When the receptionist said that the office had two cancellations, she spoke. "I'm sending my employee, Beth Zook. She needs her ribs X-rayed. They may be broken."

"Do you want us to send the bill to you?"

"Ja, please." Hanging up, she smiled softly at Beth. "Okay,

they have a cancellation and can see you in twenty minutes. Doctor Stone's office. You know where it is?"

Beth thought. "Ja, over on Second, right?" She finished pinning her dress up.

"Ja. That's the one. When you're done, come back and give me the report. If you don't have broken ribs, you can work the rest of today and this week. Otherwise..."

Not for the first time, Beth felt a strong anger toward John. "Denki." Turning, she hurried out.

***

At the doctor's office, she was carefully examined. As the doctor ran her fingers over Beth's ribs, she flinched. Finally, she was taken to the X-ray department.

"Okay, Miss Zook. No broken bones, but you definitely have some strong bruising there. Take ibuprofen every four to six hours and apply an ice pack. How did this happen?"

Beth's lips were paper-dry. Licking them, she inhaled carefully. Looking at the middle-aged doctor, she noticed her blue eyes were alert and sharp. She decided to tell the truth. "My boyfriend got mad at me last night. He..."

"Hit you. Do you know that whether a couple is married or not, that qualifies as violence? And it's wrong. I don't want to pry, but what made him mad?"

"He doesn't want me to keep working at the diner. I'm a server there. My mam is a cook."

"Wait a minute…Zook. Your dad was Amos, right?"

Beth's chin wobbled as she nodded. "Ja."

"I remember now. So, you and your mother need to work to bring money in. Have you explained this to your boyfriend?"

"Many times. He doesn't care. He doesn't believe that women need to be working outside the home. I could quilt, I guess, but I earn more money faster by working as a server."

The doctor sighed. "You know that I need to report this to the state of Pennsylvania, right? I won't use names. But I'm required by state law to report every case of violence against a family member or an intimate partner."

"We have never been—"

"Intimate? That doesn't matter. I still have to report it. You can work, but I want you to tell your mother what happened."

Beth nodded. "I will." *Just not right away.*

***

Naomi sat in the back of her mother's store with Eli Yoder. "I want to see women be free to work outside the home. You know, sometimes their family circumstances make that necessary. Someone like Missus Hershberger for instance. Amy was widowed two years ago in that accident, remember?" At Eli's nod, she continued. "The only way she can make money for her and her kinder is to operate a corn maze in the fall and sell baked goods, hot chocolate or lemonade to the English tourists. Now that she's seeing Andy Stoltzfus, he's starting to give her trouble about quitting what she's doing. Has anyone invited him to our meetings? He needs to know that because Amy is singlehandedly supporting her kinder, she can't be away from her home for several hours every day. This is the only way she has to provide for them."

Eli nodded thoughtfully. Occasionally, he scribbled notes to himself. "I know who he is. He's pretty traditional Amish, and I think he needs to be at our meetings. I'll go and explain Missus Hershberger's situation to him and invite him to start taking part in our meetings. I happened upon them last week as she was leaving the market. He was trying to argue with her so she would quit. He just doesn't see that she has very little beyond what she earns from the tourists. He doesn't like that she and her kinder are exposed to them five days a week. He raised his voice at her and was waving his arms around. Bishop Kurtz and Deacon King are meeting with him now."

***

In his barn, Andy Stoltzfus wore a look of confusion as he

talked with Deacon King and Bishop Kurtz. "But allowing her to work is an abomination! Even worse, she is exposing her kinder to all of those English tourists, and who knows what ideas they are giving to Amy and her children?"

"We need to worry much less about that than the very real possibility that Amy and her children would have no home if you were to be successful at making her quit giving tours of her farm. You do realize that since her husband's untimely death three years ago, she is the only form of support for her family, right?"

Andy could do little more than allow his mouth to hang open. "Uhhh…well, to tell you the truth, the only thing I was thinking of is the Ordnung."

"Okay, our Ordnung, as you know isn't written. It's all oral. But, if you think about the section governing families and work, there is nothing that says wives and young, unmarried women can't work outside the home. Amy works at her home, bringing honest money in from tourists. She follows all our rules. Nothing in the Ordnung says she and her kinder can't be around the English. She has assistants who work with her and they help with her children. The youngest ones don't even see the tourists. So what is your worry, really?"

"Just…that she's violating the Ordnung in some way." Andy's large Adam's apple bobbed as he swallowed hard.

"Hannes, I'll speak." Bishop Kurtz knew just what he

wanted to say. "You say 'In some way.' But you can't say in what way, specifically. We have a peer counseling organization in Peace Valley. This group is made up of elders and Amish men and women who want to help people whose confusion and fear about women working have led to relationship issues. Now, you and Missus Hershberger aren't married, but it isn't unreasonable to think that won't happen under different circumstances.

If you rip away Amy's only form of income, she won't be very happy with you. She will begin to feel you are responsible for her loss of income…and of her home. While she and her departed husband had some money in savings before he was killed, she knows that money won't last indefinitely. Therefore, given the young ages of her children, she has chosen to work *from home*, giving tours of an Amish farm to visitors who come to Peace Valley. Before she started, she came to see me with her idea and I explained to her exactly what she needed to do to start her home business and stay in complete compliance with the Ordnung. Did she tell you this?" The bishop was well aware that Amy had not explained her discussion with him.

"Nee…well, no."

"And…why would that be?"

Andy couldn't speak. His throat had frozen, not allowing words to come out.

After waiting for several seconds, the bishop spoke. "Is it because you never gave her an opportunity to explain what she did beforehand?"

"Guhhh… Well, maybe. I was just…"

"Ja, 'concerned about the Ordnung.' Andy, from this point forward, why don't you allow the elders to do their work?"

Andy flushed, feeling shamed. Not wanting the elders to see his emotions, he looked at the ground and scuffed one shoe along the ground. "Ja, I will."

The deacon broke back in. "Andy, before we leave, I want to get one piece of information from you and make an offer to you."

Andy nodded quickly.

"Do you intend to propose marriage to Amy Hershberger in the future?"

"Well, I do, ja. But… I want to make sure it's right for both of us."

"Okay. You do that. Stop putting pressure on her. She can't leave her home to work and she doesn't want to bake or quilt. Finally, we have that group. I want to offer several sessions to you. Come to six of our meetings, try them out, and see what you learn."

"Hmmm. That's all? Ja, sure." Andy didn't seem to be aware of what he was committing to.

"There is one more thing. You know now that she has no other form of income. What she's doing complies with the Ordnung of our community. Please, Andy, stop pressuring her to quit. You say you want to continue your relationship with her. If she feels any additional pressure from you, she will stop courting with you. Do you understand?"

Andy seemed to take a long time processing what the deacon was telling him. Slowly, he nodded. "Ja, ja, sure. Whatever."

Here, the bishop spoke. "Are you agreeing just so we'll get off your back? Or because you truly understand that Missus Hershberger has no income other than what she brings in from the tourists?"

"Bishop, please forgive me. But you are making me feel guilty for looking out for the safety of Amy's soul…"

"Ach! Now, I get it! You were only looking out for her soul! Hannes, that's funny…I thought that was *our* role."

"Same here! Andy, if you have any concerns about anyone, you are to discuss them with that person one time. If they don't change what they are doing, then you come to us and let us begin working with them. It's for the bishop and me, along with our two ministers, to look out for the souls of everyone in Peace Valley. Understood? I'm concerned about your soul, too, if you are going to try and badger a young widow out of her sole source of income."

CHAPTER THREE

Andy flushed. Looking out his barn door, he sighed heavily. "Okay, ja. Whatever. I'll stop. I just don't like that she's hobnobbing with the English."

"Andy, remember that she came to us. She asked us what would be permissible to do in starting her tourism business. She wanted to be sure that she wasn't in violation of our Ordnung. I believe you've lived here from birth, meaning you know our Ordnung quite well, ja?"

"Ja, Bishop, I really gotta get back to work."

"Okay, we'll go now. But I want to see you at our next meeting. They are set up for people such as you, who have trouble understanding that the women in our community have the right to decide how they are going to make a living. As long as it doesn't violate state law, federal law or our Ordnung, we are fine with their choices. There are some men, however, who believe they need to dictate how and what women can do. It looks like you fall into that group. If you want your relationship with Amy Hershberger to go well, you'll back off and let her earn her money. Hannes? We should leave now." Clapping his hat back on his head, Joseph strode out of the barn before he said something he knew he'd regret.

***

At her farm, Amy Hershberger was finishing her baking, knowing that what she earned this weekend would allow her to pay off a big bill. "Anna, what are your brothers doing?"

"Just playing outside. They're in the yard." Anna, at seven, was Amy's assistant. She had been assigned the responsibility of checking out the door occasionally, and she took that seriously. "Mama, Mister Stoltzfus is coming into the yard!"

Amy squeezed her tired eyes closed. She didn't need this now! Sighing, she spoke. "Get your brothers inside and go into the far room downstairs. If you hear anything strange, you go to the phone house and call 911."

"Ja, Mama." Running, Anna hurried to comply.

At the loud knock on the door, Amy started. Covering the dough with a clean towel, she sighed. "Ja? Andy, I am very busy right now. I can't—"

"Amy, open the door. I just want to ask you some

questions."

Hearing the back door open, then clap shut, Amy sighed again. "We can talk through the screen here. I need to get back to my bak—"

"Amy, have I been trying to force you to quit your business?" Andy was tense and he paced back and forth.

"Well…ja, you have. I don't have very much savings left after my husband's funeral and his medical bills."

"Why did you choose to start a tourism business catering to the English?"

"Because it allows me to earn money without having to leave my house. I don't have to get daycare for my kinder. I can take care of them while I work."

"And do they interact with your customers?"

Amy knew this next answer was critical. "Only in directing them as to the parts of the farm they can go to. They know not to allow people into the house. They help people who get lost in the corn maze."

Andy stopped pacing around. Looking into the far distance, he considered. Looking at his boots, he seemed to make a decision. "Amy, did you know that the elders visited me today?"

Amy was stunned. "Nee! I didn't." She wasn't about to ask

why because she'd been thinking of breaking things off with Andy before they went much further.

Looking at her with expectation, Andy waited. He waited some more. Finally, realizing that Amy wasn't going to ask, he spoke. "They were counseling me that what you do doesn't violate the Ordnung. That you went to speak to the bishop before starting this business of yours."

"Ja, I did. I wanted to be sure that it wouldn't violate anything. I don't want to put myself or my children at risk of having to leave here."

"And? What did they say?" Andy's shoulders and neck were tense.

"That, as long as I showed the tourists how a typical Amish family lives—kind of an educational tour—I would be okay. I couldn't allow them into the house. The barn would be okay, but I'm not too comfortable with that. So, I make baked goods, snacks and seasonal beverages they can enjoy at the end of their tours. At night, I work on small Amish dolls. I buy small, wood toys for the boys. After going through the corn maze, tourists can enjoy snacks and either lemonade or hot chocolate. Andy, I really have to get back—"

"Let me in." This was said in a low growl.

"Nee, Andy. Go away." As Amy gave this order, she gasped. Bishop Kurtz was coming into her yard. She said nothing else, not wanting to let Andy know what was going on.

"Please. I just want to discuss this."

"Andy! I thought you were going to get back to work after the deacon and I left your barn!" The bishop's tone was friendly, but his blue eyes were glacial.

Andy, noticing the bishop's temper, began to perspire even though the outdoor air was cool. "I came by to...uh...discuss this issue with Amy."

"Missus Hershberger, do you want him here right now?"

"Honestly, no. I have a lot of baking still to finish, then supper to make. The kinder have their homework and baths, then bedtime because it's a school night."

"Your next tour is this weekend, right? My wife and I were wondering if we could help you out."

Amy's slender face lit up. "Ja, denki! We could always use the help!"

"We'll be here bright and early. You think of what you want us to do and we'll take care of it. Andy? I believe you were leaving with me."

Andy was frustrated. With that direct order, he had no choice but to obey. Hearing the door close and lock, he sighed. He was displeased. All he wanted to do was get to a point where Amy had no choice but to agree to marry him.

"Andy, you could see she was busy—flour all over the front of her dress and apron. She was baking. She had her kinder home because school has ended for the day. Still, there's little Anna can do yet to help her with the baking. Their help comes more on tourism days. What was your purpose for this visit? And understand that I am aware you need to get back to your…chores."

Andy was trapped. "I just wanted to…to hint at the possibility of marriage."

"In the afternoon, before harvest season has ended? How long have you been courting her?"

"Nigh on two months? Something like that."

"First of all, Andy, you are rushing things. This should be the 'getting to know you' stage of your courtship. Second, she didn't look very loving toward you. She looked frustrated. Dare I say, angry."

Andy lost all discretion here. He couldn't lose her! "Bishop, I figured that if she lost this chance, she would…" Gulping, he stopped speaking abruptly.

"She would, what? Agree, out of desperation, to marry you?" Totally frustrated himself, the bishop threw his black hat onto the grass. Striding over to pick it up before the stiff breeze could blow it away, he turned to look at Andy. "You are trying to manipulate her situation. Harm her financially." Closing his eyes, the bishop breathed in and exhaled deeply, trying to regain control of his emotions. "Understand this. All during her husband's stay in the hospital, I came to regard her as a daughter. So did my wife, along with many of us here. If they were to know what you were trying to do, they would make you leave and never let you return!

The talk that the deacon and I had with you earlier today still holds. I am going to add one more thing to that: Stay away from Amy Hershberger until you understand that she has the right to choose how she will support her family. She has no husband. And second, if she does decide to remarry, she can choose whom to marry. By trying to manipulate her financially, you are abusing her. And I have to warn you, Mister Stoltzfus, that if you continue to do so, we will be forced to discuss your actions with you. Even more, if you still don't stop, you could face the Meidung. You don't want that. Please go home right now, Andy. Go home. I'm going to be watching from the yard. Don't come back."

Feeling as though he were no higher than a slug, Andy trudged to his buggy. Climbing in, he obeyed the bishop's order and went home.

In Amy's yard, the bishop waited until he was sure that Andy had gone home. Wheeling about, he returned to Amy's house, knocking at the front door.

Seeing Anna on the other side of the screen, the bishop smiled. "Hello, Anna! I need to speak with your mam."

"Okay, but she's baking. She says she's very busy."

"Ja, I know she is. I want to discuss that with her."

"I hope you're not going to tell her she can't do this anymore. My brothers and I, we enjoy helping the tourists."

She is a smart little one. "I know. You'll be able to continue helping them. May I speak with your mam?"

Anna sighed. "Come in." She unlocked the screen door, looking outside and all around the yard."

"He's gone, Anna. I made him leave."

Anna sighed, closing her eyes in relief. "Denki. Mam wasn't happy with his visit today. Mama! The bishop is here!"

"Oh! I hope…" Amy came into the living room wiping her hands on a dishtowel. She now had a smudge of flour on her forehead.

"Mama, bend down." Plucking the dishtowel from her mam, Anna scrubbed the flour off her face. "You had flour on your face."

Amy flushed slightly. "Denki. Tell your brothers supper will be ready soon. Do your homework. Bishop, come into the kitchen."

The bishop followed her. "I am sorry for disturbing you once again, Amy. I thought I should stop by after we had our talk with Mister Stoltzfus." Looking around, he made sure Anna wasn't in listening range.

"Let me." Amy moved quietly to the hallway. Listening, she heard the three kinder beginning their homework. "They're doing their homework. What happened in your meeting?"

"Have you ever heard the term 'sexism'?"

"Ja, I have. And I do feel that what Andy has been doing is sexist. He wants to manipulate my ability to earn, take it away from me along with my right to make decisions on behalf of my children, so he can make me marry him."

The bishop was temporarily speechless. "My! You are direct. Gut! He did say that, after courting you for two short months, he is thinking of asking you to marry him."

Amy's fair skin went even paler, making her look like a brown-haired ghost. "What? Nee! I've been getting to know him and he is not what I want in a husband. He's trying to manipulate me. That's not very loving."

"Has he told you he loves you?"

Amy nodded. "He's tried. I've told him that love takes much longer to develop. I was married to the most wonderful man placed on God's earth. God decided he needed Matt. I am blessed with Matt's kinder and I take my responsibility toward them seriously. If I meet the right Amish man and we grow to love each other, I will marry him if he asks."

The bishop closed his eyes, giving thanks. "I am so relieved to hear what you said. Ja, he is trying to manipulate you. He has personally brought complaints to the elders about your business, even after we have told him that you discussed your ideas with us. For that reason, all of the elders and our wives are going to be here every weekend, helping you with the tours. Just let us know where you need us and what you want us to do. I am praying that he will get the message that way."

Amy was relieved. Anna and Joshua were seven and six, barely old enough to help her out. At five, Matt, Jr. was just too young, so she kept him with her as she worked with the tourists.

"And another thing… You won't have to pay any of us for our work. Our pay will be seeing your Amish tour become a huge success. Because, if you decide not to remarry, you'll need to establish some form of reliable income for you and your kinder. The more you can put into the bank, the better."

Amy's smile was grateful. "Denki. I hope he will get the message. But, bishop, somehow he may take his sweet time doing so."

"You just let any of us know if he's becoming a pest. Does your fence have a locking door?"

"Nee."

"I'll look around for one, bring it over and install it. Thankfully, you have a six-foot fence around your property."

"Bishop, why are you looking out for me like this?"

"Amy, all through the struggles after your husband's accident, we all came to see you as our daughter. We all feel a responsibility toward you and your kinder. Now, I think I remember who might have a fence gate. I'm going to go check and, if so, bring it back and install it." Jumping up, he left and went on his errand. Amy had finished her baking and was busy making supper for her and the children when he returned.

"Gut news! I found two gates and they will fit! Both lock. I picked up locks as well. You'll have to add two keys to your ring of keys. After I install them, make sure they are locked every time you leave and at night"

Amy's smile was grateful. "I will, denki!" Thinking, she pulled a plate out and filled it with cookies. Seeing the bishop working in the backyard, she sent Joshua out. "Tell him I have a plate of cookies for him and his wife."

After the bishop had left, Amy gratefully locked both gates. She felt somehow more secure now. Andy couldn't get into the house, unless he was able to climb a high fence.

CHAPTER FOUR

That Sunday was a Meeting Sunday. Arriving at the Lapp house for the service, Amy and Anna took the lunchmeats and pickles into the kitchen. Making sure all three of her children were with her, Amy found a seat in the meeting room. "Joshua and Matt, go sit with the boys and behave. I can watch you."

Several minutes later, Amy was confused when the boys came running back. "Why? You're supposed to be—"

"Sc-c-ary man ca-ame." Matt had begun to stutter shortly after his dat's death. Andy's intensity didn't help his speech.

Sighing, Amy looked around. She saw the deacon's wife, Lovina King, smiling at her. She shrugged, a "what can I do?" gesture.

Lovina sat next to her and began to speak. "As soon as Andy went to the men's area, Matt and Joshua scuttled over to you. I believe our kinder can sense the gut and the bad in people."

"Ja, Matt has always been wary of him. I want to thank you for agreeing to help us when tourists come to my farm on weekends. It will be such a big help."

"We're happy to do so, child."

In the men's section, Andy stewed quietly. He had seen Matt and Joshua hurry over to Amy when he came in and sat in back of them. He just wanted to be sure that they were listening to God's word! Boys needed a firm hand and male leadership. Stealing a glance Amy's way, he sighed, seeing her in quiet conversation with the deacon's wife. She appeared calm, her hands resting naturally on the boys' shoulders. Really, she was spoiling them. She should have made them return. If the deacon's wife weren't sitting next to her, he would have already gone over to her and made the boys return with him. He looked expectantly at the elders, hoping they would see what was wrong with the boys sitting in the women's section. He watched for several seconds as the elders conversed quietly. He watched their gazes sweep over the women's section, and he held his breath. But...nothing. Why didn't they see the violation? He would be discussing that with the bishop after service.

Amy listened closely as Lovina King told her about an upcoming peer group meeting. "I would have to bring the kinder."

"Ja, they are welcome! We have teen girls who supervise them while we discuss the day's topic."

"Would they be sensitive to Matt's stuttering?"

"Of course. I'll make sure of that. Is he still stuttering badly?"

"It's not as bad as right after their dat died. Only when he feels stress or is scared does it come back out. The doctor said just to work with him on breathing and spacing his words. We've even been told to allow him to sing."

"Gut! What kinds of songs?"

"Children's songs and I've chosen a few simple ones from the Ausbund. It seems to help him."

"I'll pass that on to the girls. Maybe a sing-along would help him feel welcome. During lunch, I'd like to speak with you…alone."

Amy nodded. Not looking at Andy, she knew it was about him.

At lunch, the Peace Valley women trooped out of the kitchen, bearing food and beverages for the elderly, then the men, and then the kinder to eat. When the women could finally sit down to eat, Amy was starving. Feeling Lovina King and Linda Yoder joining her, she smiled.

"Keep smiling. Andy Stoltzfus looks like a grim thundercloud. And he's coming this way. Whatever he demands, refuse it." This was Linda Yoder.

"Amy, I need to talk with you. Come." Andy's voice was a menacing growl.

"Nee, I'm finally enjoying my lunch," she started as Andy clamped his hand painfully on one shoulder. "Take your hand off me. Now."

Andy, seeing the women's gazes trained on his hand, slowly removed it, letting it fall at his side. "Why didn't you send your sons back to the men's section? That was a violation. I would have supervised them for you, gladly."

Amy had had enough. Setting her fork down, she stood, facing Andy. "Andy Stoltzfus, I am a woman of twenty-eight. I believe I can make decisions for my own kinder and do quite well at it. I chose to allow them to stay with me after Matt told me that you had sat behind them."

"What? Did he stutter in that cute way of his?"

Amy gasped at the cruelty of his words. She was speechless.

"Your boys are being raised by just a woman. They need a gut, strong man in their lives if they are going to be upstanding Amish men."

"Excuse me! Ja, I am widowed. But I am following my

husband's wishes in how they are raised—"

"Mister Stoltzfus, maybe you should go back with the men," Lovina's voice was low, but had a thread of steel running through it.

"Andy, I'm more than, what did you say? 'Just a woman?' I am their mam. I look out for their physical, spiritual and emotional needs. I will not be seeing you again, from today onward. I cannot be courted by someone so overbearing."

Andy's high color suddenly faded to the color of old canvas. "What? Are you breaking up with me? I'm the best thing that ever—" As the bishop clamped his hand hard on Andy's shoulder and neck, he startled.

"Nee, Mister Stoltzfus, you are not the best thing that ever happened to her. She married that man. Sadly, Gott took him, or she would still be married to him. Now, go. We will be by later on to discuss this issue with you."

Andy stalked away, diminished and embarrassed. Amy let out a long, shaky sigh. "Denki, bishop. I had already decided on a parting of the ways. When he said that, I was—"

"Sickened? Did I hear him say that you are 'just a woman'?"

"Ja, you did."

"Okay. We'll have a meeting with him about his actions and attitude this afternoon. Missus King? Missus Yoder? Will you be assisting Amy this afternoon?"

"Ja, we will follow her to her house and discuss her options with her there."

"Gut, because it looks like Andy just started a round of gossip." Raising his voice, the bishop spoke. "Everyone! It won't be easy forgetting what you just saw and heard here. Ja, Missus Hershberger just had a parting of the ways with Andy Stoltzfus. He brought it on himself. Now, you know that gossip is deadly…and a violation of our community's Ordnung. You can't forget it, but you can resolve that you are not going to tear down reputations by besmirching gut names. Amy, tell me if you hear that the gossip has continued."

Sitting quietly in the corner with her mam, Beth Zook marveled. "Mam, she was so strong! She didn't take any of his nonsense."

"Nee, she didn't… I hope you will take this as a lesson in what to do with John Andrews."

Beth, who had just taken a healthy sip of iced tea, gasped, choking on the drink. Flapping her hands in the air, she tried to get her breath.

Mrs. Zook whacked Beth on the back until her daughter could breathe. "Are you okay?"

"Ja, but you…surprised me."

***

"Let's go inside if you're finished. I'll ask Lizzie if we can talk privately," Lovina said.

Having gotten permission from Lizzie, Lovina led Amy into the house and a small bedroom on the first floor. "Amy, now that we know you want to be a part of our peer group, I need to ask you to be very careful. What happened earlier is likely to have angered Andy greatly."

"That's partly why I made the break publicly. If I had waited until I was at home, I could have been in danger."

Lovina, about to speak, paused. "Have you picked up on something? Or has he done something?"

"I've felt a...danger coming from him for the past few weeks. Matt began to stutter again. He had almost completely stopped. At about the same time that I realized something could happen, he began stuttering again. I listened to that."

So, he's never hit you?"

"Nee, thank Gott. If he had, I would have called Sheriff Mathis. I know how he helped with Wayne Lapp. I know we aren't supposed to involve the English in our lives, but I am responsible for my children. I'm the only—" Amy stopped speaking as she fought a sudden urge to cry.

"You would have done the right thing. It's my

understanding that the elders are driving out later today to speak with Andy."

"That does make me feel better. If he knows he's facing the ban, he may behave himself and stay away from me."

"Okay, before Lizzie needs her room back, let me just tell you that we talk about sexism in our group meetings, and what it is and how it affects us. We also talk about ways to combat it peacefully—in fact, I think we are going to use your words and actions today to demonstrate what to do and say."

Amy blushed. "Denki. But I don't want—"

"You don't want to be the center of attention. Ja, I understand."

***

Later that afternoon, the bishop, deacon and both ministers pulled into Andy Stoltzfus' yard. Jumping out of the buggy, the bishop strode to the front door and knocked.

Inside, Andy heard the knock he'd been dreading. With a deep sigh, he got up and slowly walked to the door, opening it. "Come in." He swung the door wide, though he was much more inclined to slam it shut in their faces.

The bishop, as had been agreed upon beforehand, started. "Andy, what was that at the Lapp's house? Are you aware that not even three months ago, Wayne Lapp was bent on murdering both his wife and daughter because they wouldn't quit their jobs?"

Andy had been over the entire embarrassing episode on his way home and as he waited for his visitors. Seeing his mam coming into the living room, he waved her off. "It's nothing, Mam."

"Wait a minute, Andy. I'm sure she saw the whole thing, right, Missus Stoltzfus?"

"Ja. It was…embarrassing."

"Well? You embarrassed your parents. What do you have to say?"

"I have been courting Amy Hershberger for two months now. I feel a connection to her, but I worry that her chosen…*profession* could get—"

"Stop. I believe Deacon King already spoke to you about that. Amy spoke to us. Her farm tour harms nothing and nobody. She's at home, taking care of her kinder and she is paying her bills independently."

"But I could take all that off her…"

CHAPTER FIVE

"If she wanted you to do so. She made it clear today that she does not want that. Ja?"

Seeing the discomfort of both Andy and his mam, the bishop quietly told Mrs. Stoltzfus that, if she wanted, she could leave the room.

She was happy to do so, seeming embarrassed by the discussion.

Andy's eyes filled. "I…didn't expect her to do that today. I mean, I know there has been a little strain—"

Here, the deacon took over. "Andy, I would say she was feeling more than a 'little' embarrassed or upset. You inferred, in two sentences, that as 'just a woman,' she is incapable of making decisions for and acting for her children's needs. Do you remember when Matt Hershberger died?"

"Ja. It was…a year ago?"

"More like two. Her kinder were three, four and five. Shortly after she buried him, she came to all of us with her farm tour idea. She had everything written out, down to the budget numbers. 'I don't want to be dependent on the community,' she told us. 'I want to be able to provide for the needs of my kinder and me, all on my own.' You know why?"

Andy didn't and he shrugged.

"She knew there was no guarantee she'd meet someone, either here or from another Amish community, willing and able to become an instant dat. So, not wanting to completely deplete their savings account, she conceived of the idea of her tour. Everything she planned falls well within our Ordnung.

"Now, let's talk about your attitude toward women. Then we will discuss, in detail, what kinds of consequences you could face from this—especially if you don't leave her alone. 'Just a woman.' Do you truly believe that she isn't equal to us men?"

Andy knew he had to be honest, even though his beliefs would bring anger upon him. Sighing, he stood tall. "Ja. I believe all men are superior to women. We are bigger and stronger. They need us even if they don't know it or admit to it. Amy could have quilted and earned money by taking the quilts to that quilting shop. She could have baked and sold her items on the bakery stands around here. But a *tour*?"

"Andy, who conceives the child and gives birth to it? The dat? Or the mam?"

Andy choked. "The, uh, the mam."

"Andy, childbirth doesn't tickle. It hurts something powerful. I had to assist at the birth of one of my kinder and I never saw my wife go through more pain. She tried to bear it in dignity, but I could see and feel that she was hurting. Now, who takes care of the kinder more? Mam? Or Dat?"

"Mam. As she should. Dat is in the fields, shoeing horses or making furniture." Andy spoke his beliefs proudly at first, then, feeling the keen disappointment coming off the other men, he began to feel small. But he had to stand for himself. Who else was there to rescue Amy and her kinder?

"Hannes, I'll speak. We're at that point anyway. Andy, as bishop, I am responsible for the spiritual wellbeing of people in our community. You saw Amy and decided to begin courting her. From what we understand, at first, for a few weeks, it went well. Shortly after, you began pressuring her to give up her tours. You told her that she was violating the Ordnung. Were you present for the meetings that were held for the most recent change?"

Andy didn't know what to say here. Obviously, he hadn't been there! He said as much.

"Ja, the Ordnung was last updated when you were a schoolboy. I was there. My dat was there. We made the change to employment of district wives for one reason—because, back then, a recession was making life hard for many of our families. The women came to us, telling us that their families were struggling to make it on only one income. Previously, we had given families leeway so the women could work within the home. But beginning with that time, we had to make changes so that women might work *outside* the home. To be able to do this, wives had to be in agreement with their husbands that their earnings would be used only for the needs of the family. If they decided to work at our market, the diner next to Peace Valley, or the Quilt Place, wherever. And that's the way it's been since then. So, how would Amy have been in violation of the Ordnung, in its present form?"

Andy couldn't answer, so he only shrugged.

One of the ministers spoke up. You have two choices…no, three, here. Keep on as you did today and face the Meidung. Take part in peer group meetings, or one-on-one sessions, and learn about how *outdated* your attitude about women truly is."

The deacon began speaking again. "Amy didn't care for your beliefs today. Because of that and because of how you've been treating her, she'd had enough and she decided to break your relationship off. I noticed how you were looking at her boys before services began."

Andy's look was confused. They hadn't been looking at him! Or had they? "Andy, very little slips past these old eyes. You weren't happy how, when you sat behind them, Joshua and Matt left the men's section and sat with their mam. I saw—"

Andy remembered what he'd been thinking. "I thought that they should not have been sitting in the women's section. She coddles them. I would have set them straight." At that brag, Andy stood at his full height.

"Why do you think they left the men's section? Right after you sat behind them?"

Andy shrugged, completely lost. "Why" had nothing to do with it. The only thing he saw was deliberate disobedience. But, looking at the bishop's question, he waited to answer. "I dunno."

"Andy, kinder, just like animals, have an uncanny ability to detect bad in others…"

"Me? In *me*? I'm the best thing that has ever happened to Amy Hershberger!"

"How? Why?"

Andy's laughter was incredulous. Closing his eyes, he reminded himself to treat the old man with respect. "Sir, she lost her husband two years ago. She hasn't had any man around other than me. I have been working to show the boys just how they are supposed to act. Like men."

"When you courted her, you met her family, right?" After Andy's emphatic nod, Bishop Kurtz continued speaking. "She has brothers. Their relationship is loving and supportive, which means they have spent many days and hours around their nephews. You aren't the only man influencing them. When you sat behind Joshua and Matt, I was watching them. They were minding their mam, sitting still. Then you sat behind them and they noticed it. I saw a look of...panic on Matt's face. Joshua grabbed his hand and they ran to Amy. Children, like animals, are able to sense the gut—and bad—in people.

"If you want to be a part of Amy's life, you must give her the room she needs to make her own choices. She is—"

"But bishop, she needs a man around to ensure that she does make the best decisions possible. She's a woman. She can't do that."

The bishop's breath whooshed out of his chest when he heard that. "Repeat that? Nee, never mind. Did you actually just say that because she's 'just a woman,' she can't make gut decisions? Did you?"

Andy swallowed and closed his eyes in dismay and self-anger. *Had he really said that?* Thinking back a few seconds, he realized he'd given voice to very private thoughts. "Ja."

The deacon stepped up. "Okay. That makes it necessary for

me to tell you this: You are not to spend any time with her. Wait a minute. She broke your relationship off. I forgot! Ja, you are definitely not allowed to be around her or her kinder. And this brings us to the next reason for our visit. You are running the risk of receiving the Meidung. You don't want the pain or embarrassment of that. You have been attempting to live pridefully, trying to convince Missus Hershberger that you are the only hope she has. And that isn't true. The elders and I have all decided that you have to stay away from her, beginning with this afternoon. She wants nothing more to do with you. Not now, not next month. And not ever. She is moving ahead with her life, making a living and raising her children. You are to return to your farm. And, beginning this week, take part in weekly peer group meetings, where we discuss the role of women in Amish communities. Not just the traditional roles we've always given them, but those they feel they have the potential to hold."

Andy, looking steadily at the ground, sighed. He looked up slowly, into the deacon's eyes. "And if I don't?"

"You're one step closer to a banning meeting. You aren't going to learn how to view the women here any differently until you attend meetings."

Reluctantly, Andy began to accept the inevitable. He sighed and shuffled his feet, took his hat off and put it back on. "I got farming, deacon."

"Ja. And we all have farming, farrier work and carpentry to do. We all go to the meetings, too."

"What if I can't learn to see women differently?"

"Then, first, all your relationships are going to fail. No woman wants to feel like she isn't listened to. They don't want to be overpowered. Next, as the bishop said, you're running the risk of the Meidung. We don't want to see that happen. We all prayed before coming here today, asking Gott to give us his guidance."

Andy gave a loud sigh that sounded like a groan. "How long do these meetings last? What happens in them?"

"We try not to go longer than an hour and a half per meeting. We pray, and then we discuss women's roles and how they relate to our Ordnung. Not the Ordnung of any other community, just ours. Then we talk about why it's so hard for us men to 'let' them go to work, whether they leave the house to do so or they work within the home."

"And I have to do this to avoid the possibility of the ban?" Andy's voice was skeptical.

"Ja. Exactly."

Andy modulated his facial expression, looked out over the horizon and, again, removed and put his hat back on. Sighing, he nodded. "Okay. Only because I don't want to put my mam and dat through the pain and shame of a ban."

The ministers looked at each other. "Gut decision. We will leave so you can have time with your family. I believe they may be driving up."

Andy groaned. That was all he needed.

"We'll get our horses and buggies. You let your mam know that company's here." Boarding the buggies, the elders left the Stoltzfus yard. Down the road, behind a copse of trees, they stopped. "What sense did you get from him?" the deacon asked.

"He's doing it only to avoid the ban. I'm glad you didn't tell him he'd have to go to twelve sessions, minimum."

The deacon chuckled slightly. "Me, too. It nearly came out. Ja, he needs a minimum of twelve sessions."

Back at the Stoltzfus farm, Andy was taking some grief from his brothers. "Why were all the elders here? Normally, when they all come to someone's house it means it ain't good news!"

"Amy Hershberger told me she wouldn't be seeing me anymore. I've been trying to convince her that she shouldn't be running that tour thing on her farm because of the exposure to the English every weekend. Then I asked her why her boys ran from the men's section over to her at today's service. She answered and I told her she needs a man around who'll influence her boys right, that she's just a woman." Hearing the lighter footsteps of his sisters, Andy squeezed his eyes shut. He knew they'd heard him. . .

"Andy Stoltzfus! What were you thinking? Or *were* you thinking? You don't say things like that to any woman! She has been widowed for two years. She's all on her own. I love you, little brother, but I'm also happy she broke things off with you. There's a lot about us you don't know…and if you ever want to marry a gut woman, you'd better get to know what we think and how we feel."

"But that's how dat is…"

"Nee. He isn't. He's decisive. He knows what he wants after he's thought something through. But look at Mam. She's quiet, but she's also strong and she doesn't put up with nonsense from any of us. Including Dat. Let's go for a walk. Mike, tell my parents I went for a walk with Andy, please." Gripping Andy's forearm, she pulled him off the porch and toward a small stand of trees not far from the house. "Tell me."

CHAPTER SIX

Sighing, Andy tried to think where to start. "I met Amy years ago. I was going to ask her to let me court her, but Matt Hershberger asked her first."

"Okay, do you think she would have waited for you? Or that Matt would have been her first choice? And think carefully, brother."

"Ah… I don't know. All I know is that when I first noticed Amy, she was the most beautiful girl I'd ever seen. After Matt started courting her, I dated around but not seriously. Oh, I met a few I thought would make a wonderful wife, but…they weren't Amy. Then she and Matt married."

"Is that why you've never married? Because Amy was gone?"

"Ja, I guess."

"And now that she has had to become so independent, and

she is refusing to stop her farm tour…is she still attractive to you?"

Andy didn't even need to consider. "Ja, always."

Becky, Andy's sister, sighed. "Andy, when you meet someone and make them a part of your life, you accept the gut and the bad of them. Obviously, if the 'bad' is something like killing or cheating, you can't do that. But why is supporting her family by herself such a bad thing?" Becky asked her question in just the way she had for a reason.

Andy sensed a trap but wasn't sure why. So he answered instinctively. "It isn't!"

"Okay. Then why were you after her to quit her farm tours?"

The trap still hadn't snapped shut. Andy blundered right into it. "Because she is exposing herself and her kinder to the English! She's not using gut judgment. It's up to me to show her that and make the decisions for her."

"Had you asked her to marry you?"

"Nee. Although we had been courting for two months already."

"Oh! Two months! Is that enough for the two of you to really know and trust each other?"

"I know her heart, ja. She is a good woman."

"A good woman who is exposing her kinder to unsuitable Englischers?" SNAP! The trap shut.

Andy realized too late that he couldn't respond back.

"Andy. Were you going to ask her to marry you in this year's wedding season?" Becky waited.

"Well, ja."

"After dating two months? That's awful fast. And why would you marry someone who you believe is influencing her kinder wrong?"

Again, Andy couldn't answer. Then he came up with his answer. "I was going to make her quit and tell her I'd be the support for all of us."

Becky wasn't a violent woman. But in that moment, she wanted to smack Andy upside the head. "Andy!" Her voice came out as a strangled scream. "You're not making a lick of sense!"

"Why? I make sense to me!"

"Nee, you don't! You're forcing your will and decisions on a woman who has had to learn to be very independent very quickly. If I were her, and you were courting me, I would feel very crowded in, like I couldn't breathe without asking for your permission."

"But—"

"But what? What don't you understand?"

"What is this about 'feeling crowded in' or 'being unable to breathe without asking for permission'? I never did that!"

"Oh?" Becky's eyes roved over the stand of trees as they approached. Breathing deeply, she allowed the serenity of the scene to calm her down. "So, when you kept telling her that she was 'just a woman' who couldn't make decisions…no, wait, Andy. When you told her that she needed a gut man in her life to teach her boys how to be gut men, you weren't pressuring her. When you approached her at today's meeting, telling her to make your boys go sit with you, you weren't pressuring her."

Andy ground his teeth and squeezed his eyes shut. "But she is just a woman! She doesn't know how bad the world can be!"

"Yet an accident took Matt, her husband. Where do her parents live?"

"They're…passed on, I believe."

"And where do her siblings live?"

"I dunno. Here?"

"One brother and his family live here. The rest live in settlements in other states. And she makes sure all three of her kinder get to spend a lot of time with her brother, his wife and their kinder. So they do get that male influence."

"Oh. I didn't know that."

Becky flopped onto the ground. "Oh, Andy. It seems there's so much you don't know. Like how to view women in today's world, whether it's Amish or not. Are you aware that, even in our community, women can work outside the home, if she and her husband agree to that? Amy Hershberger is widowed, so that decision was all hers. It was the choice between working and doing what she is able to do best, or having her and her kinder lose their home. Would you want that to happen?"

"Nee!"

"I'm sorry, but it doesn't sound like that to me. She has to stay at home with her kinder. If she works as a server or in the quilt shop or even at the market, she has to get someone to watch them or take them with her to wherever she's working. And I don't think there are any bosses out there who would welcome a woman's three young kinder in the job every day. She would get fired. So it does sound like you want her to fail. No, Andy, don't answer. Think about what I just said."

Feeling confused and defeated, Andy flopped down next to Becky. Did he want Amy to fail? "I don't think I do. No, I don't."

"You sound sure of yourself. Andy, be honest. Making her quit work before she even agrees to marry you means she is at risk of becoming homeless. There is only so much community support here in Peace Valley. Other families here have to pay their bills and obligations and they can't support her indefinitely. She knows that. So, she looked at all her options.

"She knew that the interest and demand from English tourists was out there. They want to learn about the Amish and our lifestyle. Knowing Amy, she wasn't going to start this without telling the elders what she had in mind. If they had told her 'no,' she would have had to settle on another form of earning money. I believe she's still paying off a large hospital bill. Her farm belonged to her parents, so she doesn't have to worry about that. Repairs, ja, and she has to worry about food and medical care for her and her kinder. Clothing, she can make, but she has to buy four pairs of shoes, fabric to make their clothes, and felt and straw hats for Matt and Joshua. That's not cheap, Andy.

"Nee, don't say anything. I want you to think about what we discussed. Learn something from it. I'm not happy with what you've been doing to her. I love you, but I'm relieved that she finally had enough and broke off your courting relationship. For the success of any future courting relationships, you need to figure out why you see women as 'less than men' before you get involved with anyone else. Ever. I'm going back to the house." Rising quickly, Becky walked home before she said anything she knew she'd regret.

Andy remained behind, shook to his core. Questions roiled his mind. *Did I really do that to her? Make her feel pressure?*

Why is thinking about our women as "just women" so bad? I've been single because I didn't want to marry anyone unless it was Amy. I can't see myself with anyone other than her, so I guess I'll just stay single. He sighed, feeling lower than he'd felt in years. *Maybe the elders were right. Maybe I should get involved in those peer classes.*

The following Wednesday, Andy walked reluctantly into the Yoder house behind Jethro. "Denki for inviting me." At the offer of coffee, he nodded, thinking he'd need it to keep from dozing off.

"We're going to get started with prayer first, then start discussing our planned topic for today. Go ahead and join the other men." Eli waved in the direction of the large living room.

Andy hid his shock at some of the faces he saw and recognized. He was also surprised at how many people were there. Glancing over into the women's section, his eyes swept over the number of women in attendance. As he spotted Amy, his gaze stopped.

Amy, seeing Andy going to the men's section, allowed her true feelings to come out in her expression—her eyes narrowed in anger and the corners of her mouth tightened.

Andy, seeing this, sighed. Dropping his gaze to the ground, he walked slowly to an empty spot on one of the benches. He prepared for a boring hour and a half.

"So, now that we've prayed for understanding, let's get started. Many of you are here because you struggle with the idea of women being equal to men. I'm not going to get biblical about this, mainly because I don't have the required understanding of the Bible." A wave of laughter followed Eli's words. "Instead, we're going to look at what our wives, daughters and mothers actually already do, beyond taking care of kinder, keeping the house, cooking and gardening. I'm going to point to several of the women and ask them to give us a list. Linda will write down responses on this easel." Eli pointed to several women in succession. As he did, they listed everything they did beyond "traditional women's chores."

"Accounting, working in the Quilt Place, feeding and watering our livestock, negotiating loan payments with the bank... Leora, anything else?"

Amy responded. "Advertising my farm tour, budgeting for the household and my business, hiring farm workers to keep the farm going, finding an English worker to create a new corn maze every year, directing helpers every weekend so tours go smoothly. I think that's it."

Most people present shook their heads in admiration of everything Amy was able to accomplish.

"Manage my mother's quilting store, advertise in the *Amish Quarterly*, set up weekly schedules and write out paychecks that Mam signs. Help with the peer group and meetings here,"

Naomi said.

"Work in the diner just outside Peace Valley so I can help Mam with expenses," said Beth Zook. Her voice was low and shaky.

Every woman or girl that Eli pointed his pencil at came back with a list of chores or tasks they did that were not considered to be "traditional." Some managed the livestock for their fathers; others were responsible for hiring helpers during planting and harvesting; one wife singlehandedly ran the dairy for the farm she and her husband owned—he was busy full-time with the crops and couldn't turn his attention to the cows.

"Okay, I think we've all gotten an eye-opening view into what our women do. Ja, some work outside the home like Lizzie, Leora, Annie and Naomi. Sometimes, it's out of sheer necessity. Other times, it's because the women and their husbands have realized that they have a gift for business or for connecting with the public.

"This isn't to say that the traditional Amish businesses that are run from home are wrong or outmoded. They aren't. If that's what works for families here, then that's what those families should do. Amy, I'm going to use your situation as an example, if you don't mind." At Amy's nod, Eli continued. "Amy was widowed two years ago. Her oldest child is seven and the youngest is five. Any traditional job she could find to support her family and farm would not be sufficient. She would have to find childcare because her mam and dat have died. She has one brother here; the rest of her siblings live out of state. What about quilting or baking? I'm sure Amy considered them."

"Ja, I did. I don't bake well enough to sell what I'd need to keep our household running. I've never been interested in quilting. It's too much sitting still for me."

"That means that her farm tour, which is pretty popular, is the best option for her. She's able to buy food and supplies, pay her late husband's outstanding medical bills and maintain repairs to the house. She buys shoes, fabric, notions and hats for her and her kinder. Amy, do your earnings get you through the month or year?"

Amy sighed. "I'm getting there. With a lot of support from people here, prayer and hard work, my earnings are going up. Eventually, I would like to hire a few teens to manage each of the stations and I could manage them. Right now, that's just not in my budget. I do get through the month, but just barely."

Hearing this, Andy swallowed a rush of shame. He really hadn't cared to consider her situation.

Eli let Amy's words sink in for a few seconds, and then he continued. "Why is it so hard for us men to see our women as capable of making decisions and running businesses and farms? Naomi, please tell us how it was when you first started managing the Quilt Place."

Naomi smiled and shook her head. "Challenging. It would have been worse if Mam hadn't exposed me from the beginning to the running of the shop. She did so much all by herself. But, when she decided to take her hours to half time, she needed someone to manage. So, I learned about managing the books, keeping the time sheets, making the deposits at the bank, writing checks for employees and to pay for supplies. I thank Gott that Mam was there to teach me and supervise while I learned."

"Do you mind telling everyone why your mam decided to step back?"

Looking at her mam, then at her dat, Naomi sighed. "Okay. Dat had a very hard time with how Mam owns the shop. He wanted her to sell it. But she knows that farming isn't predictable. A year can start out gut, and then one or two weather events can destroy the crops. That's happened to Dat, as well as other farmers here. She wanted the shop's earnings to be available in bad farming years so she and Dat could keep up with payment obligations, or if we had another emergency, we would have money available to handle it."

Naomi grew emotional at this point. "Before he got involved in our peer group, Dat believed that women should not work outside the home, much less own a store. He tried to intimidate Mam into selling, and the elders got word of it. They came to talk to him and made it clear that if he didn't stop intimidating Mam, he'd be banned. I was already involved in the peer group, so I convinced him to try it out."

Many of the men who were there for the first time had come under promise of bad consequences if they didn't stop trying to keep their wives or fiancées from doing what they needed or wanted to do to earn money. Hearing Naomi's soft, emotional words, most of them felt ashamed.

"Denki, Naomi. Lizzie, how is Wayne doing?"

CHAPTER SEVEN

Lizzie sighed. "He has gut days and bad. Right now, the bad days outnumber the gut ones. We go to see him one day a week, and he's trying to understand why it's not bad for us to be 'out there,' working around other people. I was able to make quilts at home, and then sell them on consignment in Annie's store. That helped us while Wayne was laid up with his arm injury. It also helped that every carpenter here stepped up and helped fill all his orders—and they're continuing to do so!"

"Lizzie, if you don't mind, would you reveal just why Wayne is in the Mennonite-Amish mental health hospital?"

"Ja, because I think it's a lesson to everyone here, whether they are man or woman. My gut husband experienced years of child abuse at the hands of his dat. He witnessed his dat beating his mam. His mam escaped, leaving all the youngest kinder with their dat, probably because she sensed he was about to kill her. Once she left, his dat's only outlet for his anger and abuse was…the kinder. "That's what he grew up knowing, so I don't blame him for what he believes. He is working hard to change that, but it will be a while before he can safely come home. The psychiatrist and psychologist have told Leora and me that he suffers from something called PTSD. It means post-traumatic stress disorder. He can be fine one minute, and the next, something will happen around him and it's as if he's back in a moment where he's being abused or hearing his mam being beaten.

"Ladies, he did beat me. The elders came to talk to him, and for a while he really tried. But, the last time he went backward he was in the market, and he overheard shameless gossip about why Leora and I were not living in our home. And all his fears and those old ghosts came back. That's when he began planning how he would kill us. He completely lost his grip on reality then. I'm not making any excuses for him. He was wrong, and now he's paying for that." Lizzie sat down, her heart pounding.

The room was so quiet that a mouse could have twittered and it would have sounded loud. Linda Yoder stood and approached the front of the room. "Lizzie, denki for telling us such a hard story. I do have one question that everyone here should know the answer to, so they can put Wayne's situation into perspective. Why was his dat so abusive of his mam?"

Again, the silence descended into the room. Andy felt it and his gaze centered on Lizzie, who stood once again.

"I understand this only secondhand from Wayne. His dat came from a very conservative Amish sect and believed that no woman should get the opportunity to earn money, even by working from home. His wife was desperate to earn what she needed to escape, so with the few extra dollars she had, she bought baking supplies. Other wives in the community sold her goods for her and then took the money to her. She was able to hide it from Wayne's dat. Also, he believed that women should not speak up unless spoken to. He was raising his daughters in the same way. Wayne told me that he knew their dat abused his sisters as well. And that they are abused to this day by—" Lizzie couldn't continue. She collapsed onto the bench and Leora wrapped her arm around her shoulders.

Linda grabbed a box of facial tissues and gave them to Leora. "I'm sorry for bringing up something so painful, Lizzie, but it's important that everyone here know just how far sexism can be taken." She turned toward the entire group, men and women. "Because that's what women are facing, is sexism. That simply means that men and society believe that women should take care of 'women's chores' only. That they aren't good enough, smart enough or strong enough to own, run or manage a business. Ladies, since you were all fourteen years old, you helped your mothers or your fathers to run their own home-based businesses, right? And you learned what you needed by being exposed to what your parents did. That was gut training for your own lives as married women, ja?"I want us to take a break now. We have coffee, lemonade and cookies ready for everyone. Men, think about what the women have said here. We'll come back in ten minutes for the last half of our session."

The group broke up, moving to the kitchen for the mentioned snacks. Andy toyed with sneaking out, but seeing Bishop Kurtz's eyes trained on him, he sighed, gave up on his idea and grabbed a fresh cup of coffee. Sitting on the bench again, he thought. Realizing it was too noisy, he decided to go outside. "Bishop, I'll be in the back yard. I need to think for a few minutes."

"I think I'll join you."

Andy sighed yet again. Plopping himself onto the back porch swing, he sipped the hot coffee. *I can see where Amy had to make the decisions she needed to make. I made some bad mistakes there. Ja, Lizzie needed to find a gut job so she could keep the household running. I see that. But this thing about 'if women want to work outside the home, they should be allowed'? I don't know. . .* He turned his head at Deacon King's call. Slipping back into the kitchen, he poured another cup of coffee.

Eli approached the front of the room. "Men, I want you to think about where your beliefs come from. Your parents? Conservative Amish communities? Or even English communities? Because the English struggle with this, too. Right now, there is a conservative strain in government. I agree with much of that, but not the parts that say a woman shouldn't earn a salary equal to a man's. Using Annie's words, she wanted to have the protection of the store supporting them if Caleb, like other farmers, had a bad farming year. He can't control the weather. It took him some time, but Caleb now supports his wife's store, knowing that it's a protection for their family as well as a way for Annie to have her own creative outlet.

"Another new member here is Beth Zook. She came by herself for this meeting. She is struggling with her own beau, but I won't get into the particulars. She and her mam work in the diner just outside Peace Valley. Her dat died, so it's up to her and her mam to earn what they need, as cook and server, to keep their home from being taken by the bank. *They have no choice. They have to work.* Quilting or baking wouldn't meet their financial needs. Beth, may I reveal just a little more information?"

Beth nodded slowly.

"Thank you. Beth's beau is pressuring her to quit her job. He tells her she shouldn't need to do any work at all. Now, his dat and mam came from a very conservative Amish sect out of state. We know where John gets his beliefs. We are working to get him to join our group and see why his beliefs and demands of Beth won't work. And I don't want anyone gossiping about

Beth's situation. If I hear of anyone doing so, I'll inform Bishop Kurtz."

Linda stepped up again. "Today's discussion question is, "Is it right for men to tell women whether they can work, or where they can work?" Break up into groups of four, please, and discuss that question. One person should be group recorder and write down everyone's beliefs. We'll discuss them in…twenty-five minutes."

The noise level in the room went up. Eli opened the back door while Linda opened the front, allowing some of the sound to escape.

Andy found himself in a group with Deacon King and Jethro Yoder. When the group's recorder pointed at him, he sighed. "I believed it was right for me to tell women where and when they could work. After hearing some of the situations here, I realized that I didn't know enough of each family's situation to judge."

"Who are we to judge?" This was Deacon King.

Andy's mouth opened and closed as he struggled with that. "Ahh, well, we are on this earth to make sure that women are safe. To make sure they use good judgment in the—"

"Wait," Jethro said. "We have pretty smart women who live and work here. I trust their judgment just fine. If my dat were to die, I would grieve him and miss him. But I would know that

Mam could keep our home and business running. She was encouraged and taught by her parents. Andy, I've helped Amy out with her farm tour. I saw a confident young woman making decisions and directing volunteers where they needed to be. The tour ran smoothly, with tourists moving from one station to another, fully enjoying themselves. Before they left, Amy made sure they enjoyed snacks. And, by the end of the day, she had entertained and taught over fifty tourists by my own estimate. She does that every weekend, and in between she prepares for the upcoming tour, which takes planning and coordination. She knows what she is doing. Ja, she is 'barely breaking even.' But she isn't relying on the generosity of the families here, is she?

"Ahh, nee. But shouldn't someone, a male, be guiding her decisions, to make sure—?"

"Ach, the 'judgment' question again. Andy, if your dat were to pass away today, would you trust your mam to keep the house and farm running?" Deacon King sat back, waiting patiently.

The question and topic hit Andy hard in the gut. Breathing deeply, he took a swallow of coffee and considered. "While she would need some help with some farming aspects, I believe she could keep everything running. But—"

"Nee, Andy. Leave judgment out of it. She has been running your household for, what, thirty, forty years, right? I'm sure your dat handed all that over to her. Consider the household and budget to be a small business. How long has it been since she's made a mistake that affected how the house functions? Or does she go running to your dat for every decision?"

Andy allowed his gaze to go outside. Seeing the leaves falling off the trees, he felt calm once again. "I can't think of a time when she's made a poor decision. The only time she and Dat confer on a decision is when they have to talk about a large expenditure. You see, they make decisions together for bigger money expenditures."

"Okay, can you see your household being operated like a small business, with your mam as the boss?"

Closing his eyes, Andy tried to imagine this. "I don't know. Maybe."

"Andy, can you see someone like Annie Miller, opening her own business outside the family home? Running it successfully with the goal of having it be a protection against a bad farming or carpentry year?" Jethro looked into Andy's confused gaze. "I know this is a strange new way for you to think. But you need to change how you view women and your relationship to them."

"Clearly, if I am not to keep fouling up my approaches to them," Andy growled.

"Andy, do you know where your views on women come from? Because I've always seen your mam as quite independent. And I never got the impression that your dat didn't want her to do anything, like work in the market or another business selling retail goods." Deacon King leaned forward, his coffee cup in between his knees.

"Nee. Dat has always encouraged Mam to do what she felt she needed to do." Andy paused, thinking back. "I remember…back when I was, maybe eight, ten years old, I met a boy. We were only friends for a short time. Mam and Dat let me spend the afternoons at his house before it was time for chores. After a while, I began to pick up on his dat's attitude toward women and girls. 'You're stupid. You can't do nothing right. Don't expect to be allowed to work outside the home because girls and women don't have the judgment to even work at the market without messin' up.'"

"But, Andy, if your dat didn't have those beliefs, how would it make sense for you to assume them? He would have had more of an influence on your thinking."

"Ja, that's why I can't understand why I think that way."

"Andy." Eli dropped into their group. "How does your dat express himself toward your sisters?"

"Protective. He is protective."

"Okay. And? Anything else?"

"Wait." A dim memory began surfacing. "I remember that

my oldest sister said she wanted to work a shop. Dat was reluctant, for some reason. Being that I was only twelve, I had to be upstairs in bed. But I had heard their discussion before I went upstairs, so I snuck over to the top of the stairs and listened to my sister and Dat. She wanted to work in an English store that specialized in selling Amish creations. 'I can do this, Dat. It'll allow me to save money so that Ben and I can start our married life out on the right foot.' Then my dat disagreed. He said that my sister didn't have the head for numbers and books. 'You'd do better makin' quilts here at home and selling them. Or baking and spending a day or two selling to other Amish and to the tourists.'

"My sister was hurt, and she asked him why he didn't believe in her. Well, that slowed my dat down and he told her he did believe in her. 'But I've always just seen you as soft and more suited for the home arts.' In the end, my sister didn't apply for that position. She does quilt and she does a great job at it. Her work is in demand and what she earns is a nice supplement to Ben's carpentry work."

"What did your dat say about your other sisters?" Eli was astounded.

"He had no objection to their working in that store. When Annie opened her quilt shop, they worked there for a year or two before they began having babies."

Eli thoughtfully pulled at his beard. "You know, putting

myself in your oldest sister's shoes, I would be hurt. What was her reaction when your younger sisters were able to get the permission she sought?"

"Angry and hurt, ja. She loves Dat, but that has put a strain in their relationship. And she has forgiven him…but has never forgotten what he said and decided."

Deacon King broke in. "And this had its effect on how you see Amy Hershberger?"

Andy had clearly never thought about it from that point of view. "Huh?" He took his hat off and scratched his full head of hair. "Huh! I never saw it that way."

"Think carefully and answer as honestly as you can. Why do you believe that Amy could use bad judgment? Or that she's made a mistake with her choice?" Eli watched Andy closely.

Andy did as Eli directed. He took his time and thought of both women's situations. He compared both women to each other. He thought about the decisions his sister had made and realized she had made very few significant ones. Nor had Amy. "Uh, well, they are both gentle in their personalities. Soft, you know? But strong. They both have a core of strength that, with their faith, gets them through the tough times. I guess—nee, I know—that I mistook that gentle personality as being too soft to survive out in the world. Hearin' that Amy is able to direct others during tours so every one of them is successful surprised me. It shouldn't. She's able to make a decision and stick to it. A lot like my sister."

"And about the risk of bad judgment?" Eli wasn't going to let him wiggle out of that one.

"Bad judgment... I still have a hard time believing that having tours every weekend and allowing English tourists to be around her kinder is good."

"Okay, let's go with that. Do you distrust the English?"

"Some, ja. I don't know that they wouldn't try to hurt the children."

"Amy has thought of that and taken precautions. Do you trust her ability to protect them?"

"Oh, ja!"

"Then, if she can protect them, having tourists around shouldn't be an issue, especially now that so many of us are volunteering to help her during her tours. It's that many more extra pairs of eyes to supervise the kinder, ja?"

Andy couldn't deny that. "True." A question occurred to him. "Do you think she'd let me volunteer?"

CHAPTER EIGHT

Deacon King leaned forward. "Let me ask her. But after Sunday's meeting, she was pretty mad. I wouldn't get my hopes up. I think you've burned your bridges pretty thoroughly with her."

Andy had known that instinctively, but hearing the words still hurt. He drew in a big breath, trying to minimize their impact. "Ja, I got it."

The group work came to an end and each group's recorder reported the results of their discussion of the question. "Okay, it looks like some of the men here still believe that women shouldn't work outside the home, even if the wife has the ability and aptitude to do so. Men, we still have some work to do. Those of you who still have this belief, please raise your hands. Ja, you'll identify yourselves, but we are going to at least understand that this belief comes from a sexist view of the women here. That way, when the question comes up in your families, you're better prepared to give your wives or fiancées the benefit of the doubt." The meeting ended and the participants went home.

Andy went home with questions swirling around in his head. That night, after supper, he asked his dat whether he truly believed women should work outside the home if they had the desire and ability to do so.

"Ja, now I do. I regret saying what I said to your sister. I thought I was protecting her and doing the best thing possible for her. I've watched her operate her quilting business over the years. She has done a great job, setting rates, ordering, making her quilts and receiving payment. There was only one customer who cheated her out of what she was owed. Your sister figured out what mistakes she made and hasn't made them again. Ja, she is a gut business woman. Today, I would say that if she wants to work in a store or office, she should do so, as long as her husband agrees. If she wants to start her own business, she should, with his agreement."

"Dat, I made a similar mistake with Amy. Only now…"

"Son, I saw what happened. Ja, she's a woman, but she is making that farm tour business work. I hear she has volunteers helping her out now."

"Ja. It is working and the volunteers are a big help for her."

"You miss her, ja?"

"Ja. But I was stupid. She won't want to go out with me again because I didn't trust that she had the ability to make the decisions and carry them out."

"Son, I am sorry. Like me, that's your burden to bear. Keep that in mind as you look around for another young woman to court."

"Dat, I don't think…"

"What?"

"I always imagined myself courting and eventually marrying Amy. Then, she married Matt Hershberger and I was ready to be single all my life. None of the other women here—"

"Stop. Don't be stupid. There is a young woman here or in another community that is right for you. Allow yourself time to grieve, then start noticing who's out there."

"But, dat—"

"Andy! You acted poorly around her and tried to order her around. You learned your lesson. Now, get yourself out of the muck and resolve to do better next time. You going to those peer group meetings?"

I went to this one. It was…okay. Not sure if I'll go to more."

"Well, I'm going. And you'll be with me."

Andy stared at his dat, his jaw fully dropped.

***

While Andy was having his discussion with his dat, Eli and Deacon King were discussing him. "Eli, you think he's learned that he has sexist ways of thinking?"

"It's occurred to him. If he's smart, he'll allow himself to figure out how to change that so that when he meets someone new, he won't blow that relationship."

Hannes stared at Eli. "You know, you sounded just like an Englischer there."

Eli chuckled. "Ja, remember, my family and I spent some years living in an English town. I picked up on some of the lingo."

Hannes' laugh came out as a bark. He shook his head. "Apparently! Were you able to maintain your Amish lifestyle and beliefs?"

"Ja, we were. I was there with my mam and dat. He had to work in a factory to earn the money he needed to pay off a bank loan. Once he was able to do that, he took the rest of his savings and we moved here and found our home."

"Back to Andy Stoltzfus. I think he'll learn more readily. Losing Amy was a real shock to him. John Andrews, on the other hand…"

"Ach! From what I've learned from Beth, his beliefs are rooted in extremely conservative thinking. When we have time, I think we should have a conversation with John's mam. I'll bring Lovina along with me so she might feel more comfortable."

"When do you have time?" Eli was thinking of his schedule for the next two weeks."

"No time like the present. Do you have any time tomorrow?"

"I have three shoeing appointments tomorrow. One early, the other two mid-afternoon and early evening. You?"

"I have to go to the lumber store and pick up a large order along with some other supplies. I want to take care of that early as well. What time do you anticipate being back home after your early appointment?"

"Probably around nine in the morning."

"Perfect. Go with me to the lumber store, we'll unload the wagon and store everything in my shop. Then we'll go to the Andrews farm."

"I like that. But no appointment?"

"Nee. I don't want to give her time to think of potential answers to anything we might ask. Our group has become well-known here."

"Ja, it has. Okay, I'll wait for you and we'll go from your house."

***

It was almost ten the next morning when Hannes and Eli finished unloading the lumber and supplies in Hannes' carpentry shop. Lovina was with them as they discussed what they would ask Mrs. Andrews.

Hannes began. "I met with Beth Zook a week or two ago. She had a bruise on the side of her face that John had given her. We talked about it. He had ordered her to quit her job serving at the diner and she told him why she couldn't. He took it personally, thinking that she was defying him."

"She is taking part in our peer meetings and says they are helping her."

"She doesn't speak out much or volunteer any information," Lovina said. "I get the sense she's frightened of him. She's also desperate because she has to keep her job so she and her mam won't lose everything. I spoke with her privately and she seemed more comfortable with that. She was actually able to admit that she was thinking of breaking off with John. She even said that she'd rather be an old maid than marry John if this is how he's going to treat her."

Eli listened, soaking everything in. "Has she met his parents?"

"Ja. She says his mam is like a scared little mouse. She says nothing without deferring to her husband. That makes me wonder—"

"Getting his approval before saying anything, along with being so fearful could be a sign that he has abused her. But until we see for ourselves, we should not assume," Hannes pointed out. He went on, seeming to mutter to himself. "It makes me wonder too, but until she is ready to say anything, there is little…but maybe…could it happen?"

Eli sent a puzzled glance over to Lovina, who smiled and shook her head. "That's how he does his best thinking. He figures things out by talking to himself. It's actually very effective for him."

"We'll have a discussion with Missus Andrews, and then decide who would be best able to work with her and her husband. It may be one of us, or maybe one of the elders and his wife, depending on how Mister Andrews responds." Eli rubbed his whiskery chin, thinking.

***

Arriving at the Andrews place, Deacon King knocked on the front door and they waited.

Inside, Big John waved his wife back to her kitchen work. "I'll get it. You get back to your work." Swinging the door open, Big John's surprise caused his jaw to drop. "Deacon!

Missus King. If we would have known you were coming, we would have had a pie ready! Come in! Enter!" Big John's voice was energetic, but Eli's finely trained ears picked up on the thin thread of anger running underneath.

"Denki! I need to introduce Eli Yoder to you as well. We have some business to discuss with you…and your wife." Hannes gave Big John no room in which to refuse to allow his wife to participate in the meeting.

"Okay, come in. Emma, make a pot of coffee, now! Do we have any pie left from yesterday?"

Emma's voice was whispery-quiet. "Ja, I'll make coffee. We have some pie left. Please, sit."

The guests sat, and after enjoying a few bites of the pie, they came to the reason for their visit. "We need to speak to the two of you individually. It's about the peer community group and its work here. We're trying to reach out to every family in Peace Valley."

"John, if you'll come outside with the deacon and me, we can get started so you can get back to your own work. I know your time is valuable." Eli rose.

"It's not necessary for my wife to speak up. I speak for her," John said.

Hannes tipped his head to the side. "Why is that?"

"Women don't have the judgment to speak about some matters. It's for their husbands to communicate for them."

Seated, Emma Andrews flushed and crouched over as she heard what her husband said.

Lovina rose and faced John directly. "I'll take my chances. Being 'a woman,' I may be able to pick up on what Emma says."

John understood Lovina's message. Flushing and scuffing the floor, he shrugged, mumbling. "Okay, whatever."

Outside, the men sipped their hot coffee gratefully. The mornings were becoming chilled, and hot beverages were more and more comfortable.

"So, what's this meeting for?" John was off-balance. He didn't like this feeling, and he sought to get information so he could regain control of the situation.

"We simply want to learn about your family. Who's the head of the home and how family decisions are made. What are your beliefs about family roles? Kinder? Your wife?" Deacon King purposely asked about John's wife at the last because he wanted him to think that her position wasn't as important as the other family members' roles were.

Big John was in his element. Feeling comfortable, he settled himself comfortably on his seat, gripping his coffee mug between weathered hands. "Oh, that's easy! Our family follows conservative, traditional Amish beliefs. The husband and dat is the head of the household. He makes the decisions and everyone follows his decisions and directions. Our kinder know their place in our family and they do what I tell them. I raised my sons to be strong men, respectful of Gott and ready to be the heads of their own households when they married. I'm still teaching that to John, my youngest. He's learning well."

Eli and Hannes waited for John to mention Emma.

"John, what about Missus Andrews? What's your wife's role?" Eli deliberately didn't ask whether she took part in the decision-making process.

"We discuss things important to the family. *I* make *all* the decisions and she goes along."

"She has no input? She doesn't tell you what she thinks or give you her opinions?"

"What opinions? She doesn't need them. What's important is my opinion on any given question. She's supposed to obey me, and that's all."

Hearing these words, Eli suppressed a sudden shiver. *I feel sorry for the womenfolk in this family.* Swallowing his coffee, Eli wet his mouth. "Has she ever worked outside your home? Say, at the market or the diner, as a server?"

"What! Nee, no way! Women don't have any business, workin' away from the family home. It's for their husbands to earn the family's income. Period! Is that what this meeting's for? You want my wife to be able to go traipsing out there and work?"

"Nee, John, and you know better," said the deacon. "We are visiting every family to find out what the dynamics are. If any families are interested in adding extra income through the wife, we help them achieve that goal. If not, then that's fine."

John sat back again, relaxing. "Okay. Just so you know, Emma isn't allowed to work out there. She has plenty to keep her occupied in our house."

Inside the house, Lovina worked gently to get Emma Andrews to explain how things ran in her household. "Do you get to make any of the decisions, say about a big expenditure?"

"Oh, nee!" Emma's voice was still whispery-quiet, but she was more comfortable around Lovina. "John doesn't believe wives have any business making decisions."

"Well, what about working, maybe from home? Quilting or baking, and then selling your work to earn money for the household?"

"Nee. I'd have loved to quilt and sell them to tourists. John told me nee."

"Was that all he said, or did he say or do anything else?"

Lovina felt her heart hammering in her chest as she waited for Emma to respond.

Emma waited for several seconds to answer. "He got…so angry at me. He was yellin', hollerin' and picking things up because he wanted to throw them at me. But the kinder were all in the kitchen with us, so he couldn't."

"Oh, my! I need to know this. Has he ever hit you or thrown things at you before?"

At this question, Emma's eyes filled with tears. "Ach, I'm sorry!" She looked quickly toward the closed back door, not wanting John to see her crying. Inhaling quickly, she regained control of her emotions. "Ja. He has hit me in the past. That seems to have stopped now that it's only John at home with us. Now, all he does is yell, order me around and throw things when John is gone."

"You grew up in the same conservative community as John, ja?"

"Ja."

"Did your mam work, either baking and selling her cakes and cookies or by making and selling quilts?"

"Ja, my dat actually said she could. He knew that as a farmer, he was never assured of a good farming year, and he knew they could put the money from her quilts back as emergency savings. And I expected I would be able to do that when I married John."

CHAPTER NINE

"But it never happened, did it? What happened in bad farming years for your husband?"

"A lot of worry—anger and worry from him. Strict budgeting. I got very gut at… Would you like to go out to the front and walk?"

Lovina immediately agreed because she knew Emma was going to tell her something important.

Outside, Emma continued. "I got very gut at pinching pennies and dollars in good harvest years. I hid the money and when the harvests were bad, I had that money to fall back on. I used a lot of coupons and made less-expensive meals. Still, sometimes we fell behind on bank loans. One year, the bank repossessed one of John's farming tools. He was so mad. He blamed me, telling me that I should have somehow been able to come up with extra money in the budget. Missus King, that beating was bad. I ended up in the emergency room, with a broken rib and a broken nose."

Lovina shook her head, feeling sick. She felt blessed, having Hannes as her husband. "Emma, you can call me Lovina. I want to offer you the opportunity to take a place in our peer group meetings."

"Nee, oh, he won't let me go! He never lets me use the buggy unless he's with me!"

Lovina was stunned. It took a few minutes for her tongue and throat to work again. "You mean you can't go out by yourself, without him being with you? Does he go shopping with you? What about quilting frolics?

"He goes shopping with me, but only when he can spare the time from farming. And frolics? I haven't been to one since I got married. John believes that women should not be anywhere their husbands are not."

"Emma, he's putting a very strict interpretation on our Ordnung. There's nothing in there that says wives or girlfriends can't work, and nothing that says wives can't enjoy participating in a quilting frolic. He's…he's abusing you when he hits you and even when he yells at you. When he doesn't allow you to attend social events or go shopping by yourself, he's isolating you. This is so you can't gain strength to resist him. And, by not allowing you to work, he is abusing you financially and telling you that you aren't gut enough or smart enough to hold down a job."

Emma was only able to open her mouth. Nothing came out. Then, "But. . . John, he loves—"

"Maybe. But he isn't showing that in a very gut way. Emma, too many of our men here are stuck in what is called a sexist way of thinking."

"'Sexist?'" Emma was shocked, and she began to feel angry. "Missus King, are you talking of...matters that better belong in the bedroom?"

"Nee! Sexism only means that men think that women aren't good enough to make significant family decisions, hold jobs, earn money or even make decisions about whether they will go to a quilting frolic. For all of your marriage, John has ruled you, telling you how things would be—because he believes you aren't smart enough or even good enough to do so."

Emma, who had been ready to order Lovina to leave her husband's house, closed her mouth. Sitting back on the porch swing, she pulled her shawl more closely around her shoulders. "Oh. But I am good enough! I run the household, even though I let him think he does. I budget the money and even squeeze out money here and there for emergencies."

Lovina nodded emphatically, nearly dislodging her head covering. "Ja, gut! Gut! I *knew* you had it in you! I would really like to see you at our next peer meeting. My husband and Eli

Yoder are trying to convince your husband to attend as well."

Emma pursed her lips, pushing them out from her teeth. Shaking her head, her still-beautiful eyes grew sad again. "Nee. He will never agree to attend a meeting where the topic goes in direct disagreement with his beliefs."

"Hannes and I will pick you up, then. At the least, you can learn what we are struggling against. And you can get some new knowledge about how to regain some of the equality in your marriage to John. Simple things, like salting away a few pennies, quarters and dollars, against financial emergencies, allowing him to think he is the one running the household. You don't have to be obvious about it. Continue agreeing with him—but, where and when you can, quietly do what *you* know to be right. If he tells you not to buy fabric to make new clothes, but you know you can't repair your existing clothes anymore, buy the fabric anyway. Store it away while he's working in the fields. And, while he's working, sew your new clothes. If you make a new shirt for him, tell him you had fabric left over from a year or so ago. If you take part in a community meeting where someone is facing the Meidung, you don't have to vote in agreement with him, when you know the person's actions don't rise to that level. Vote differently."

Emma was silent, thinking about everything Lovina had just advised her to do. "I need time to think. This Sunday is a Meeting Sunday, ja?" At Lovina's nod, she sighed. "I will tell you what my decision is. At lunch. When is your next meeting?"

"Next Thursday. Emma, there is one very important reason I want you to participate. Your son, John Junior, has been dating Beth Zook. And—"

"She is such a sweet girl. It's just too bad that to keep their home she and her mam have to work so hard at the diner."

"You understand. Gut! Because your son has been pressuring her to leave that job. I suspect she has told him that she has to work so she and her mam don't lose what they have—their home and everything in it. Money must be a constant struggle for them. I strayed off topic. I'm sorry. In trying to convince her to quit her serving job, your son has used physical pressure. In the same way your husband has threatened and hit you, John Junior has hit Beth."

Emma gasped, feeling physical pain. "Nee! No!" She gasped again, knowing her voice could carry. With difficulty, she moderated her tone. Then, she thought back to several incidents where John Junior had taken the same attitudes and actions as his dat. Weeping, she pulled a facial tissue from her apron. "It's true. I know that. I have seen him using the same actions that John, my husband, has used against me. Yelling. He has also thrown objects at me, trying to intimidate me. And my husband has said nothing to him."

Lovina was afraid for Emma and Beth. "Listen, we need to

finish quickly. Beth is already a group member. She's learning so much! That's why I want you to participate as well."
"I'll think about it and let you know Sunday at lunch."

"Denki. I hear the men inside. We'd better get inside ourselves." Lovina rose and delicately helped Emma to rise. She felt protective toward the older woman, instinctively seeing her as more delicate. *Nee, Lovina. If she has survived John's treatment this long, she is much stronger than you think.*

"Wife, why were you outside?" John felt suspicious, feeling that something was up.

"We wanted to enjoy the fall air as we talked about the Ordnung."

Lovina had stayed quiet on purpose, wanting Emma to give direction. "Ja, John, I learned so much from her. Now that I know you grew up and met in a conservative district, I understand your position. Are we done? I need to start dinner and begin preparations for supper. I also need to make more progress on that quilt for my customer."

"We're finished. Eli?"

"Let's go. John, Emma, denki for opening your home to us." Clapping his felt hat on his head, Eli led the way out. He had a lot to say. In the buggy, he leaned forward, looking across Lovina to Hannes. "Let's go to that diner first. The one where Beth works. We need to talk, and I didn't want to be around

John or Emma."

"Ja, we can go for a while." Hannes changed the horses' direction, making their new destination the diner.

"Lovina, what did you learn?" Eli was curious.

"He beats and intimidates her and has never allowed her to make a decision about their household. He doesn't even allow her to go shopping by herself or go to a quilting frolic! Because he doesn't believe Emma should be anywhere he isn't." Lovina's voice quivered, betraying her anger.

Drawing in a deep, calming breath, her gaze moved from bare trees to quiet farms as they approached them. Feeling calmer, she spoke again. "But she has a core of strength even he hasn't seen. She allows him to think he makes all the household decisions. She has, somehow, found a way of squeezing out a little money from the shopping budget and putting it away for emergencies. And she's thinking about coming to our meetings. She'll let me know after meeting on Sunday."

"Oh, my, it is bad there. Eli, do you think we'll have to hide Emma for her protection?" Hannes was worried.

"I don't know. Lovina, John is still refusing to attend the meetings, which makes me wonder if their son will." Eli finished speaking as they pulled into the diner's parking lot.

Inside, Hannes sat next to Lovina while Eli sat opposite them. "Gut morning, Miss Zook! We would like three coffees and, for me, a slice of your mother's apple pie. Lovina, Eli?"

Lovina ordered cookies and Eli, peach pie.

Beth hurried off to get their orders.

"Miss Zook, we have a small piece of gut news. Missus Andrews may agree to attend our meetings. She will let us know on Sunday."

Beth sagged in relief. "My boss gave me a short break. May I join you?"

"Please do! Lovina, why don't you explain what you learned?"

"Beth, just like John has been treating you, his dat treats his mam. She has managed, somehow, to survive all these years of intimidation and mistreatment. She also allows him to think that he makes every decision for their household. What this does about your decision regarding staying with John Junior, I don't know. But we felt you should know."

"That it comes from what he's seen and experienced. Ja. His anger has been out of proportion to the situation, many times. That will make my decision much easier to make. I don't want to live as Missus Andrews has for all these years. Before my dat died, I remember seeing him treating my mam with love and tenderness. He treated me and my brothers and sisters with love. Ja, when we were bad or did wrong, he was angry. But he never abused us. We would get one swat on our fannies and that was it. If he and Mam argued, they settled it like adults. And they made up. That's what I remember, and that's what I want when I meet the right man. I thought John would be the right man. But, it appears he isn't."

Lovina put her hand on Beth's forearm and hand. "Beth, my girl, I regard you almost as one of my own daughters. I feel protective toward you. Don't take too long in making your decision."

Beth sighed. Lovina's hand on hers felt gut. "Ja. His anger has been growing. When he…hit me the last time, I thought he had broken my ribs. I hurt for days! Mam took me to the healer and she gave me some herbs for the pain. I'm better now—no pain at all."

"Excellent. Now, if John's mam joins our group, we will be teaching her about sexism and how it affects the women here." The discussion continued for several minutes until the group paid and went home.

***

While the peer members were meeting with John's dat, mam and Beth, John Junior was working. As he did so, he ruminated on the distance he sensed between him and Beth. As he considered it, he grew angrier and angrier, thinking of what he could do to teach Beth a lesson. He was especially angry that he still hadn't been successful in forcing Beth to quit her job. *She's supposed to quit, stay home and do what good Amish women do! They aren't supposed to work outside the home. They aren't allowed to!* Unable to come up with a workable solution, he decided to talk to his dat about it. *He's been able to make Mam do what she's supposed to do for all these years. He'll have the answers.*

That night, after supper, John asked his dat if they could talk about something. "I need some answers and guidance, Dat. I figured you would be the best person to guide me."

John Sr. smiled. These words stroked his ego. "Certainly. Let's go to the barn. Wife! Make more coffee, now!" John snapped his fingers.

CHAPTER TEN

Emma scurried to obey her husband. Then, knowing that her husband and son wanted to talk in the barn, she filled a large Thermos. Once they left, she closed her eyes in relief. *Finally, a few minutes free of orders!*

In the barn, Big John turned to his son. "What's on your mind?"

"Dat, I have seen how you handle Mam and my sisters. I admire you for it, for standing true to the Ordnung we lived under in Ohio. I have been ordering Beth Zook to quit her job at the diner, but she has refused. I've used some of your…*methods* to try and convince her, but still, she holds onto her job. I need your guidance, dat."

"Sit, son, sit. It's clear to me that you are the one child willing to hold true to what Gott has told us. I am going to explain to you just how I have gotten your mam and even your sisters to obey me when I tell them something. You see, I reinforce my orders to them with physical action when they are...what's a gut word? *Resistant* to what I tell them to do. Years ago, before we had to leave Ohio, your mam expressed a desire to work to bring additional money in for our family. I was stunned! She didn't think I was earning enough, and she wanted even more! I told her nee, of course. She told me that all she wanted to do was bake and sell the goods for extra money for food. 'We have four kinder and maybe more, if Gott wills it. If I can earn a little more, I can buy more groceries. Or I can quilt.' I told her nee again. That I was the head of the household and my earnings were perfectly sufficient. She seemed to accept my decision as law. 'Seemed to,' John, because not three years later, she brought up the same bad idea. 'Husband, the weather wasn't kind to the crops this year. The harvest was—' and that's when I delivered my reinforcement, son. I backhanded her when she wouldn't stop crying about 'we need money.'

"Unfortunately, I hit her hard enough that she had a big bruise on the side of her face. She had to stay home from Sunday meetings for about a month. I learned after that to hit her only hard enough to get my decision across to her. Or I hit her where the marks wouldn't show."

"Dat, I confess, I... I did the same to Beth when she refused to quit her job at the diner. But she is still working!"

"Ach, she is a stubborn woman, ain't? Then, that's when

you deliver such a harsh physical punishment that she *can't* work—for weeks. She gets fired, and you get your wish. If she dies after you deliver your punishment…oh, well. You had to teach her a lesson."

As John was telling his son how he kept his wife and daughters under his control, Vernon King happened to be walking by. Hearing the ugly topic under discussion, Vernon stopped and listened. When he heard Big John tell his son to deliver a "harsh physical punishment," that was when he got scared. When he heard John brush off the possibility of Beth's death, he tiptoed away as quietly as he could. When he was a good distance from the barn, he ran home.

***

"Dat! We have to talk." Vernon bent over, gasping and trying to get his breath back.

"Son, what is it? You look scared!"

"Dat, I just overheard John Andrews—the dat—telling his son how to get Beth Zook under control." More gasps. "He said…he told John to beat Beth up so badly that she wouldn't be able to work for weeks. 'She gets fired,' he said. Then he said, 'If she dies after you deliver your punishment, oh well'!"

Hannes sat down, his legs refusing to hold him up. "Son, sit down here. This coffee should still be warm. Here." He shoved the thermos over to Vernon.

Vernon drank deeply of the still-warm coffee. "Dat, what are we going to do?"

"Tell Eli Yoder and the other elders. Then, you and I are going to go talk to Sheriff Mathis. We cannot allow this to be carried out. We would be condoning murder. Let's go tell your mam where we're going and why." Locking the shop, Hannes and Vernon hurried into the house.

"Lovina! There you are. Vernon and I have to go meet with Eli and the elders. Vernon, tell your mam what you just told me."

Vernon repeated what he had heard.

Lovina went pale and her eyes widened. "Oh my, no! Ja, go. I'll go to the diner. Beth and her mam may be working. I'll warn them both."

"I'll hitch the second buggy for you. Be careful! If you see either of the Andrews men, steer clear of them."

"Ja, Hannes, I will." Lovina took Hannes' and Vernon's hands and squeezed them. "*You* be careful."

***

In town, Hannes and Vernon, along with Eli and the other elders, jumped out of his buggy and strode into the sheriff's office. "Ja, we need to speak with Sheriff Mathis, if he's available."

The deputy behind the desk was wide-eyed. It was rare for the Amish to request a meeting with law enforcement. "I'll go see if he's available. Take a seat, please."

The men only had to wait a minute. Sheriff Mathis came out quickly. "Hannes, Joseph, I take it today's visit isn't social. Would you all come into my office?"

In the closed office, the Amish visitors sat or stood. "Sheriff, my son, Vernon, overheard something. Vernon?"

Again, Vernon repeated his words. "I think they're serious, sir."

"It sounds like it. Joseph, what do you think? I know you don't encourage violence or the use of weapons. Handle this situation the same way we handled the Lapp situation?"

Looking at the elders and Eli, everyone nodded. "Ja, we all think that's best."

***

Sheriff Mathis visited Joseph Kurtz at his home. "Joseph, have you heard of anything that tells you where John Andrews will be spending time with Miss Zook?"

"We spoke with Beth. She told us that she has agreed to a meeting with John. It will take place this coming Saturday night. She says that John likes to stop at a popular picnic spot, with tables. You know which one?"

"There's several. Is there one in particular your community members patronize?"

"It's the one about a mile-and-a-half away from the Andrews home, off state road twenty-three. It's just south of town."

"Oh, yes, I know which one you're talking about. Okay. What time do they generally get together?"

"She said he'll pick her up at about seven, after she's had time for supper with her mam and time to clean the kitchen."

"I'll have my deputies positioned close by, but not visible. You know, we're going to have to alert Beth's mother."

"Really? I was praying we wouldn't. She and Beth have been through so much since her husband died."

"We have to. Once we move in and grab Beth, we're going to take her straight back home. When she sees people she doesn't recognize, she's going to get worried. And if John is able to do any harm to Beth, she may need medical attention. Again, her mother will have to know so we can take her to where Beth is being treated."

A knock sounded at the door. "Let me answer that. It's Eli, his son Jethro and the other elders." Loping to the door, Joseph answered it. "Come in. John Mathis is here and we are starting to work on particulars."

"I think that would be an excellent idea." The sheriff had spoken up. "Beth and her mother are going to be shaken up and they'll need all the emotional support they can get. Is Beth's mother seeing anyone?"

"Not that we know of. She's been so busy with work, just trying to survive."

"Agh, poor woman! It just irks me when men think they can order women around to puff up their own egos." The sheriff grumbled as he thought about Beth's situation.

Finally, the plan was approved. "Okay, everyone, Sheriff Mathis will run this just as he did the situation with Wayne Lapp. His deputies will be dressed like us. Sheriff, we need to know how many men and how many women, and their approximate sizes so we can loan you Amish clothing. We will meet at the picnic grounds close to the Andrews home. Beth knows this, so she will suggest it to John."

The sheriff took over. "We want to move in as soon as it looks like Andrews is going to get violent. Allow my deputies and me to take care of that. You stay in the background. It's much safer that way."

"Would it be helpful if one or two of the wives approach Beth when it looks like things are going to get, well, difficult?"

Eli really wanted to help.

"No, that will only put them at risk of physical harm, especially if John knows he has been outed."

"'Outed?' What does that mean?" One of the ministers was confused about the term.

"I'm sorry. That just means that he's been found out and we're going to stop him. He will be even angrier and may try to take his anger out on Beth. We don't want that. It could also put other women in harm's way. This guy sounds like he's not afraid of hitting a woman to make his point or get his own way."

"Sheriff, what will happen to John's dat? And his mam?"

"Well, since Vernon reported that he overheard John's father plotting to harm Beth, we will send uniformed deputies to their home to arrest him. Is his wife participating in your meetings?"

"Not yet. We're working to make that happen, and she told us she would let us know at our next Sunday meeting. She really fears him. Whatever he orders her to do, she does."

***

Over the next few days, the elders met with Eli, Vernon, Jethro and the sheriff's office. Amish clothing changed hands and the final plan came together. "We'll meet at the picnic grounds at five p.m. I want a few of your community members to be there, doing something like a quiet celebration or something."

"Maybe we can make it look like a group meeting before it gets too cold. You know, in the next month, it will get seriously cold before winter starts."

***

Finally, the day arrived. Various people in Peace Valley and outside the Amish community woke up knowing that at the end of the day lives would change.

John woke up, and after breakfast he went with his dat to clean up the fields after the harvest. "Dat, was it a gut harvest?"

"It could have been better, son. Much better. But, with Gott's guidance, we will get through this winter. Let's begin cleaning up the chaff and the stalks left behind." Four hours later, sweaty and dirt-covered, the men came back into the house. "Wife! We're going to clean up. I want dinner in thirty minutes!"

"Ja, husband. It will be ready. I've been working on it." Emma scurried around, brewing coffee and heating vegetables. The beef potpie bubbled in the oven. Emma stirred some potatoes on the stove, checking them for doneness. She had already set the dessert on the counter, where it cooled.

Upstairs, Big John finished wiping the caked dust off, washed his face and combed his hair back. He put on clean clothing. Walking into his son's room, he saw that John Junior was doing the same. "Son, where are you taking Beth tonight?"

"She wants to go to the picnic grounds and just enjoy the evening, she said. What she doesn't know is that I am giving her my final ultimatum. She quits her job, and she goes home uninjured. If not…" John's voice was quiet, but not quiet enough.

Emma had quietly come upstairs, planning to tell the men that dinner was ready. Overhearing John's voice, she stopped in the hallway. Knowing what he meant, she covered her mouth and wheeled back around. As small as she was, her steps didn't make much sound. Still, she was cautious, avoiding parts of stairs that she knew creaked. Wringing her hands and pacing, she wanted to do something, but knew she couldn't. *But maybe…* She was jolted out of her musings by the noisy footsteps of her husband and son. "Dinner's ready." She was nervous, not wanting them to see that she knew what they had been talking about.

Neither man noticed Emma's nervousness. Instead, they dug into their meals, eating silently after their prayer. "What's for dessert?" Big John wiped his face and whiskers clean of his lunch, waiting.

"Apple crisp with ice cream. Here you go." Emma's hand

trembled slightly as she handed them their bowls. "More coffee?"

"Ja." John wolfed down his apple crisp and indicated he wanted a second serving. He waited as Emma hurried to comply. "Son, we should get back outside. It's a bit cool out there today."

"Ja, but it'll feel gut." Without thanking his mam for the delicious dinner, John walked out with his dat.

***

After picking Beth up at her house, John drove her to the picnic area. Lifting the small basket she had prepared, he took it to the nearest table.

Beth glanced around, half-hoping to see signs that help was close by. She closed her eyes briefly when she saw the Yoders and Millers at the far end of the picnic area. "This looks gut. I'll spread the tablecloth so our food stays clean." She quickly snapped the oval tablecloth out and spread it over the concrete table. Removing the jars of spreads, bread, cheese and sliced meats, she invited John to sit.

John made a thick, hearty sandwich for himself. "Mmm, this is gut. So, have you made a decision? When will you quit working at that diner?"

Beth sighed. She had hoped to delay this part of the evening.

"John, can we enjoy our meal for a few minutes, then talk about that?"

John looked deeply at Beth. "I would like an answer. Tonight." His voice deepened."

"Ja, I know. I will let you know, but I just want to enjoy a little supper and time with you first."

John couldn't see anything wrong with that. "Okay. This time." After finishing two large sandwiches, he dug into half of the cookies Beth had packed. Without thanking her, he burped loudly, and then took a large slurp of coffee. "Well?"

Beth took her time. Wiping her mouth and setting her napkin down, she sighed. "John, Mam and I are by ourselves. Other than the small amount of savings Dat was able to set aside for us, we have nothing. Mam needs my earnings to keep us in the house so the bank doesn't foreclose on it. Oh!"

John had slammed his meaty hand on the table in anger. "You know what I want! You know I want a wife who stays at home and doesn't work. She should only take care of the house and our kinder!" Rising, he moved around to Beth's side of the picnic bench. Grabbing her by the arm, he pulled her up and tried to pull her away from the table.

Beth tried not to resist. Still, her foot caught on the high, concrete foot of the bench. As John tugged at her arm, she tried to free her foot. Her leg and foot twisted painfully as he pulled on her arm. Nearly horizontal, she was unable to balance so she could pull her foot free. Feeling her leg twisting, she heard a sharp snap as the bone broke. "Ach, John, you hurt me! Let me go, now!" Beth's voice was shrill.

Hearing Beth's exclamation, the deputies surrounded the couple. They had moved closer as John grabbed Beth's arm. He hadn't noticed their presence.

"John Andrews, let her go!" One of the deputies stood close behind John, handcuffs in his hand.

John, turning, didn't recognize the faces. "Who are you? This is a private matter."

"Not when you hurt her, it isn't. Deputy, cuff him." Sheriff Mathis read John his Miranda rights. "We need a second set of cuffs. He's too big for one set."

Beth, lying on the picnic table by now, breathed deeply, trying to stave off nausea. She was angry. "John, we are not a couple anymore. I am not leaving the diner and I am not marrying you!"

"What? I'm your only—"

"Nee! I'd rather stay single!"

"Take this disgusting weakling away." The sheriff's voice was disgusted.

***

Weeks later, the peer group had made headway, signing up several new couples shaken by Beth Zook's beating. The group's main focus continued to be discussing and teaching sexism and its effects on Amish families.

THE END.

THANK YOU FOR READING!

I hope you enjoyed reading it as much as I loved writing it! If so, look for the next book in the series at your favorite online booksellers in ebook for paperback format.

In the meantime, you can learn a bit more about my free digital starter library in the next chapter. And if you've missed any of books, check out Also by Rachel Stoltzfus and pick up any books you've missed at your favorite online booksellers :)

Best,

Rachel

RACHEL STOLTZFUS

A WORD FROM RACHEL

Building a relationship with my readers and sharing my love of Amish books is the very best thing about writing. For those who choose to hear from me via email, I send out alerts with details on new releases from myself and occasional alerts from Christian authors like my sister-in-law, Ruth Price, who also writes Amish fiction.

And if you sign up for my reader club, you'll get to read all of these books on me (in ebook format):

1. A digital copy of **Amish Country Tours**, retailing at $2.99. This is the first of the Amish Country Tours series. About the book, one reader, Angel exclaims: " Loved it, loved it, loved it!!! Another sweet story from Rachel Stoltzfus."

2. A digital copy of **Winter Storms**, retailing at $2.99.

This is the first of the Winter of Faith series. About the book, Deborah Spencer raves: " I LOVED this book! Though there were central characters (and a love story), the book focuses more on the community and how it comes together to deal with the difficulties of a truly horrible winter."

3. A digital copy of **Amish Cinderella 1-2**. This is the first full book of the Amish Fairy Tales series and retails at 99c. About the book, one reader, Jianna Sandoval, explains: " Knowing well the classic "Cinderella" or rather, "Ashputtle", story by the Grimm brothers, I've do far enjoyed the creativity the author has come up with to match up the original. The details are excruciating and heart wrenching, yet I love this book all the more."

4. A digital copy of **A Lancaster Amish Home for Jacob**, the first of the bestselling Amish Home for Jacob series. This is the story of a city orphan, who after getting into a heap of trouble, is given one last chance to reform his life by living on an Amish farm. Reader Willa Hayes loved the book, explaining: " The story is an excellent and heartfelt description of a boy who is trying to find his place in the community - either city or country - by surmounting incredible odds."

5. A digital copy of **False Worship 1-2**. This is the first complete arc of the False Worship series, retailing at

99c. Reader Willa Haynes recommends the book highly, explaining: " I gave this book a five star rating. It was very well written and an interesting story. Father and daughter both find happiness in their own way. I highly recommend this book."

You can get all five of these ebooks **for free** by signing up at

FamilyChristianBookstore.net/Rachel-Starter

Or via TEXT MESSAGE send

READRACHELS to 1 (678) 506-7543

ENJOY THIS BOOK? YOU CAN MAKE A BIG DIFFERENCE

Reviews are the most powerful tools in my arsenal when it comes to getting attention for my books. As much as I'd love to, I don't have the financial muscle of a New York publisher. I can't take out full page ads in the newspaper or put up billboards on the highway.

(Not yet, anyway.)

But I have a blessing that is much more powerful and effective than that, and it's something those publishers would do anything to get their hands on.

A loyal and committed group of wonderful readers.

Honest reviews of my books from readers like you help bring them to the attention of other readers.

If you've enjoyed this book, I would be very grateful if you could spend just 3 minutes leaving a review (it can be as short as you like) on this book's review page.

And if, ***YIKES*** you find an issue in the book that makes you think it deserves less than 5-stars, send me an email at RachelStoltzfus@globalgrafxpress.com and I'll do everything I can to fix it.

Thank you so much!

Blessings,

Rachel S

ALSO BY RACHEL STOLTZFUS

Have you read them all?

AMISH SEEDS OF CHANGE SERIES

Struggle. Resentment. Love.

Book 1 – Amish Seeds of Change

Amish teen, Emma Lapp has had a lifelong struggle with weight. Worse, Jacob, the man she wants desperately to court with only sees her as a friend. Caught between the loving excess of her mother's care and the desire to make a change, Emma feels overlooked and left behind. But when a terrible accident forces Emma to face hard truths about herself and her relationship with her sister, will this be enough for Emma to seize her dreams? Read More.

Book 2 – Amish Courage to Change

After Emma Lapp's weight loss surgery, her sister, Barbara, will do anything to make her sister fail. Tempting foods. Too large portions. But with the support of her long-time friend and true love Jacob, Emma perseveres. Seeing Emma's success, Barbara risks her marriage and her sister's good name in one, final act of ultimate betrayal. Will Barbara succeed in driving her sister away? Or will Emma find the courage to change herself, her family, and her community? Read More.

Book 3 – Amish Time of Change

Coming July 2017 – Get notified the moment it's released when you join Rachel's Readers Club at http://familychristianbookstore.net/Rachel-Starter.

AMISH OF PEACE VALLEY SERIES

Denial. Redemption. Love.

The Peace Valley Amish series offers a thought provoking Christian collection of books certain to bring you joy.

Book 1 - Amish Truth Be Told

Can the light of God's truth transform their community, and their husbands' hearts? Or are some secrets too painful to reveal?

Book 2 - Amish Heart and Soul

A lifetime of habit is hard to break, and for one, denying the truth will put not only his marriage, but his life, at risk. What is the price of redemption? Can there truly be peace in Peace Valley?

Book 3 - Amish Love Saves All

Can the residents of Peace Valley, working together, truly move past antiquated views in order to save themselves? (In Kindle Unlimited until 6/26/17)

Or SAVE yourself a few bucks & GET ALL 3-BOOKS in 3-Book Collection.

LANCASTER AMISH HOME FOR JACOB SERIES

Orphaned. Facing jail. An Amish home is Jacob's last chance.

The Lancaster Amish Home for Jacob series is the story of how one troubled teen learns to live and love in Amish Country.

BOOK 1: A Home for Jacob

When orphaned Philadelphia teen, Jacob Marshall is given a choice between juvie and life on an Amish farm, will he have the strength to turn his life around? Or will his past mistakes spell an end to his future?

BOOK 2: A Prayer for Jacob

Just as Jacob's life is beginning to turn around, his long, lost mother shows up and attempts to win him back. Will he chose to stay go with his biological mom back to the Englisch world that treated him so poorly or stay with his new Amish family?.

BOOK 3: A Life for Jacob

When orphaned teen Jacob Marshall makes a terrible mistake, will he survive nature's wrath and truly find his place with the Amish of Lancaster County?

BOOK 4: A School for Jacob

When Jacob's Amish schoolhouse is threatened by a State teacher who wants to sacrifice their education on the altar of standardized testing, will Jacob and his friends be able to save their school, or will Jacob's attempt to help cost him his new life and home?

BOOK 5: Jacob's Vacation

When Philadelphia teen, Jacob Marshall goes on vacation to Florida with his Amish family, things soon get out of hand. Will he survive a perilous boat trip, and Sarah the perils of young love?

BOOK 6: A Love Story for Jacob

When love gets complicated for Jacob, what will it mean for his future and that of his new Amish family?

BOOK 7: A Memory for Jacob

When anger leads to a terrible accident, will orphaned Philadelphia teen, Jacob Marshall, regain the memories of his Amish life before it's too late?

BOOK 8: A Miracle for Jacob

When Jacob Marshall makes a promise far too big for him, it's going to take a miracle for him to keep his word. Will Jacob find the strength to ask for help before it's too late? Or will pride be the cause of his greatest fall?

BOOK 9: A Treasure for Jacob

When respected community leader, Old Man Dietrich, passes on, Jacob discovers that the old man has hidden a treasure worth thousands on his land. Can Jacob and his two best friends solve the mystery and find the treasure before it's too late? Or will this pursuit of wealth put Jacob in peril of losing his new Amish home?

SIMPLE AMISH LOVE SERIES

Friendship. Betrayal. Love.

The Simple Amish Love 3-Book Collection is a series of Amish love stories that shows how the power of love can overcome obsession and betrayal. Join the ladies of Peace Landing as they hold onto love in Lancaster County!

BOOK 1 – Simple Amish Love

She's found love. But will a stalker end it all?

After traveling for rumspringa, Annie Fisher returns to her Amish community of Peace Landing ready to take her Kneeling Vows and find a husband. And when handsome Mark Stoltzfus wants to court with her, it seems like everything is going to plan. But when a stalker tries to ruin Annie's relationship, will she be strong enough to stand up for herself? And will her fragile new romance survive?

BOOK 2 – Simple Amish Pleasures

A new school year. A new teacher. A hidden danger.

Newly minted Amish teacher, Annie Fisher is ready to start a new school year in Peace Landing. Having been baptized over the summer, Annie is excited to begin her life as an Amish woman. And when the Wedding season arrives, she and Mark will be married. But there is a hidden danger that threatens everything Annie wants, everything she's worked for, and everything she loves. Can Annie face it, and if she does, will it destroy her?

BOOK 3 – Simple Amish Harmony

She's in love. With the brother of the woman who betrayed her best friend.

Jenny King is elated with her new love, Jacob Lapp. But a cloud hangs over their developing relationship. Jacob's sister betrayed Jenny's best friend, Annie Fisher and has now been cast out of the church. What happens next could spell the end of Jenny's future plans, and the simple harmony of her dreams.

Or SAVE yourself a few bucks & GET ALL 3-BOOKS the Collection.

AMISH COUNTRY TOURS SERIES

A widow. A new business. Love?

Join Amish widow, Sarah Hershberger as she opens her home for a new business, her heart to a new love, and risks everything for a new future.

Book 1: Amish Country Tours

When Amish widow, Sarah Hershberger, takes the desperate step to save herself and her family from financial ruin by opening her home to Englisch tourists, will her simple decision threaten the very foundation of the community she loves?

Book 2: Amish Country Tours 2

Just as widow, Sarah Hershberger's tour business and her courtship with neighbor and widower, John Lapp, is beginning to blossom, will a bitter community elder's desire to 'put Sarah in her place' force her and her family to lose their place in the community forever?

Book 3: Amish Country Tours 3

Can widow Sarah Hershberger and her new love John Lapp stand strong in the face of lies, spies, and a final, shocking betrayal?

Or SAVE yourself a few bucks & GET ALL 3-BOOKS in the Collection.

AMISH COUNTRY QUARREL SERIES

Friendship. Danger. Courage.

Join best friends Mary and Rachel as they navigate danger, temptation, and the perils of love in the Amish community of Peace Landing in Books 1-4 of the Lancaster Amish Country Quarrel series.

BOOK 1 - An Amish Country Quarrel

When Mary Schrock tries to convince her best friend Rachel Troyer to leave their Amish community and move to the big city, will a simple quarrel spell the end of their friendship?

BOOK 2 – Simple Truths

When best friends, Mary Shrock and Rachel Troyer, are interviewed by an Englisch couple about their Amish lifestyle, will the simple truth put both girls, and their Amish community, in mortal peril?

BOOK 3 – Neighboring Faiths

Is love enough for Melinda Abbott to turn her back on her Englisch life and career? And if so, will the Amish community she attempted to harm ever accept her?

BOOK 4 – Courageous Faith

Before Melinda Abbott can truly embrace her future with her Amish beau, Steven Mast, will she have the courage to face the cult she broke free of in order to pull her cousin from their grasp?

Or SAVE yourself a few bucks & GET ALL 4-BOOKS in the Collection.

WINTER OF FAITH

Hardship. Clash of Worlds. Love.

Join Miriam Bieler and her Amish community as they survive hardship, face encroachment from the outside world, and find love!

BOOK 1: Winter Storms

When a difficult winter leads to tragedy, will the faith of this Ephrata Amish community survive a series of storms that threaten their resolve to the core?

Book 2: Test of Faith

When Miriam Beiler, a first class quilter, narrowly avoids an accident with an Englischer who asks her for directions to a nearby high school, will this chance meeting push Miriam and her Amish community to an ultimate test of faith?

Book 3: The Wedding Season

When another suitor wants to steal John away from Miriam, who will see marriage in the upcoming wedding season?

Or SAVE yourself a few bucks & GET ALL 3-BOOKS in the Collection.

FALSE WORSHIP SERIES

A dangerous love. Secrets. Triumph.

When Beth Zook's daed starts courting a widow with a mysterious past, will Beth uncover this new family's secrets before she loses everything?

SAVE yourself a few bucks & GET ALL 4-BOOKS in the Collection.

AMISH FAIRY TALES SERIES

Cinderella. Sleeping Beauty. Snow White.

Set in a whimsical Lancaster County of fantastic possibility grounded in strong Christian values, join sisters Ella, Zelda and Gerta as they struggle to find themselves and their places in a world fraught with peril where nothing is as it seems.

SAVE yourself a few bucks & GET ALL 4-BOOKS in the Collection.

OTHER TITLES

A Lancaster Amish Summer to Remember

When troubled teen, Luke King, is sent for the summer to live with his uncle Hezekiah on an Amish farm, will he be able to turn his life around? And what about his growing interest in their neighbor, 16-year-old Amish neighbor Hannah Yoder, whose dreams of an English life may end up risking both of their futures?

ABOUT THE AUTHOR

Rachel was born and raised in Lancaster, Pennsylvania. Being a neighbor of the Mennonite community, she started writing Amish romance fiction as a way of looking at the Amish community. She wanted to present a fair and honest representation of a love that is both romantic and sweet. She hopes her readers enjoy her efforts.

CPSIA information can be obtained
at www.ICGtesting.com
Printed in the USA
LVHW080858060620
657562LV00021B/343